THERE WERE GIANTS in the earth in those days; and also after that, when the sons of God came in unto the daughters of men, and they bare children to them, the same became mighty men, which were of old, men of renown . . .

—*Genesis 6:4*

HERE IS WISDOM. Let him that hath understanding count the number of the beast: for it is the number of a man; and his number is six hundred three score and six . . .

—*Revelations 13:18*

STUART J. BYRNE

THE ALPHA TRAP

MAJOR BOOKS • CANOGA PARK, CALIFORNIA

MAJOR BOOKS
21335 Roscoe Boulevard
Canoga Park, California 91304

First printing. . . . . . April, 1976
Second printing. . . . . April, 1978

Printed in the United States of America

ISBN 0-89041-194-8

Three hundred and sixty days of sunshine per year had stamped this section of the Mojave with the inimitable mystique of typical desert wilderness—sweeping concave seas of baked sand and sage misting into time-frozen pre-Cambrian tides against naked and subtly distant ranges which were somehow beautiful in their dreaming sorrow; eternally haunting the wanderer with their purpled mirage of secrets to be told when Man was dead.

Here, south of Death Valley and west of Baker, was the restricted Fort Irwin military reservation. For some years now a tracery of jeep, "six-by" carrier, Euclid, Tournapull, and crane tracks, had pointed from Fort Irwin across the sands and flash-flood *bajadas* to a simple landmark which was known to cartographers as Drinkwater Springs. Slightly beyond this point of reference was an inconspicuous ten-acre area that had been fenced off and posted as "radiation contaminated." This was a ruse to arouse an instinct of self-preservation in any chance trespassers, for the simple reason that the sand-camouflaged "deck cover" would not support a man with certainty.

When the State Department's Army-converted YHC-1 helicopter lowered toward the center of the fenced-in area, acres of "sand" dropped away miraculously into a huge well-shaft. Per the Goldstone tracking station, this was timed within twenty-three minutes before the latest Soviet spy satellite would rise above the horizon. Up from the cavernous depths rose an entire flight deck of the type used on the largest aircraft carriers. Antlike figures of signalmen waved bright flags. The big copter settled easily onto the vast deck, and the entire structure lowered rapidly. The "sand" canopy rolled back into place above the visitors, and

5

to right and left of them the girders and floor plates of level after level flashed upward.

The "Tank" on level J-sub 1 was also known as the Scenario Room. Buried beneath the bottom level of the entire installation, it was so heavily shielded that the Tech Corps had concocted a legend for it: "Only God or a very educated electron could even crawl through the coax linkages. . . ." Of course such materialistic views were merely the farthermost landmarks of a limited empirical science. Just how far lead shielding, ECM interference and ion-plasma "shell" chambers could go in counteracting so-called *psi*-phenomena was a moot point. At least the complex hatch-and-tunnel routine for getting into Omega's ultimate Sanctum Sanctorum was sufficiently exotic to satisfy the psychological needs of a standard power ritual.

Some of the less-endowed representatives of the Joint Chiefs were smugly impressed by a mother-pat sense of super-security; whereas the more light-endowed were sobered by the conviction that *nobody* really had a fix on the situation—and as far as God was concerned, His switchboards appeared to be over-saturated with the issue of rice and beans. The world was FUBAR with its Russian Roulette of population explosions, energy crises, Third World insurrections, and runaway inflations—but all were parlor games compared to the fact that Armageddon had entered, snickering. . . .

∞

Lights dimmed in the Tank's small amphitheater. The panel rasters warmed up. Coded signal patterns flashed. Each panel viewer had four small screens, a built-in TV, and voice pickup. Beyond the panel banks in a wall-sized well or recess, a canted map of the world became visible under black light. In Northern California, a red light suddenly gleamed at them. At all positions, monitor 1 came into focus. Five charter members of Omega's secret "Lodge" stared back at them. With their chairman and chief, John Anthony

6

Hart—now present in the Tank—they were known simply as The Council; but between them they represented a sizable chunk of the Free World's technical-industrial capacity, not to mention enough financial muscle to stagger the money markets of the world.

On the world map, Washington blinked red. For each viewer, monitor 2 came to life and four members of the U.S. Senate Security Committee faced them. London blinked red, and each monitor 3 lit up with the proper face and form of the MI-7 Chief, tweeds and all.

Twelve hours prior to this moment an Omega Condition Three had gone out. In accordance with a two-nation ultra-secret "scenario" covering this incredible contingency—it was tantamount to saying "in case of devils"—a handful of pin-sized diodes, in three widely separated time-sharing computers, gated the octal logic which triggered a gigantic defense linkage. The global tendrils of emergency connections were data-linked, micro-waved, and satellite-relayed far and wide into maximum-security cabler units tied in to "Project Genesis."

Across the United States, millions of slumbering citizens were unaware of subtle electro-mechanical movements in hundreds of ICBMs resting in their silos as warheads were remotely armed. From its underground bastion in Colorado Springs, NORAD obediently alerted SAC, without yet knowing the objective, while thousands of National Guard posts and police/sheriff headquarters throughout the nation wondered what was up. They were suddenly on standby for invoking Martial Law at a moment's notice, wherein the most specific feature was to be an *absolute* blackout of the Press. Panic was the main thing to watch for in case of an information leak, but few men on Earth knew that the thing called "X" was the other chief factor in the crisis equation; X was now prime target. To "somebody" out there it could even be worth the risk of World War III, or Armageddon itself.

But *if* the probe came, the highest knowledgeable echelons of the world were *still* not ready. Certainly if the traditional layman in any part of the world had known what was going on that following day, beneath the timeless face of the Mojave Desert, there would have been a mass wandering in the streets, a panic migration to the hills, or a total collapse of Wall Street—among many lesser evils.

∞

"I don't like it, J.A.," came the clipped voice of Senator Cain from monitor 2 while addressing John Anthony Hart. "Your boy isn't cleared for an action of this magnitude."

"That's in case of snafu," snapped Hart, a small, leathery dynamo of inexorable causality. "If somebody taps his brain he won't *know* what we know—at least not about *X*."

"We hadn't thought, over here," interjected MI-7 with a Balaklava tone of commitment, "that a 'snafu' factor would be considered in this operation. Where will Dr. Brockway be?"

"Right next to my *boy*, as Cain prefers to call him," retorted J.A. "Look, gentlemen, David Duqayne is very close to me . . ."

"*Too* close," interrupted the senator. "In fact that's one of the reasons why I'll be at the Westhaven hearing."

J.A. ignored him. "I'm practically using him like bait in a tiger trap. But it's the triggering point we've got to have!"

"Small price," said Cain, "for all the panic he's caused."

"But there's his motivation—he wants to prove his point! Of course we have to take the stand that he's pretty spaced out on the Kettleridge matter, but actually his whole ingenious plan has provided a possible chance for a breakthrough. He doesn't know it, but Omega will be standing in the wings for this performance."

8

"Not to mention some of our own intelligence," added Cain.

"This is too much of a blur for me, J.A.," complained a Pentagon general. "I can't find a peg to hang my hat on. What's the hard core of it all? Where are these way-out scientists in your outfit? What's *their* analysis?"

The prematurely gray-haired but ruddy-faced physicist next to J.A. did not wait for an invitation to speak. He addressed the monitors brisky, but with a knowledgeability and conviction that was mesmerizing in its impact. "With the Nieuwald discovery and the death of Dr. Kettleridge—I mean the *way* he died—science has virtually been scrabbling for a new model of the universe. We've practically had to scrap our psi-particle theories and junk the principle of quarks. After all, gentlemen, 'e' *does* equal mc-squared! That means that matter is energy and energy is matter. For the first time, we've been forced to face the full implications of this fact. Since bioplasma, quantum pairs, and black holes, we've been looking at the possibility of whole new systems of higher energy states—and now that X is in our hands—"

"Come on, Conrad!" urged J.A. impatiently. "Translate it for them!"

The physicist squared his shoulders and leaned forward as though bracing himself for an ordeal of revelation. "All this is saying that practically *nothing* is supernatural—there seems to be cause and effect for everything. A lot of the old semantics will have to go—like so-called 'extra-physical' planes of existence, parallel universes, other dimensions—whatever. . . . Much that we have always regarded as superstition is of course just that—*as* interpreted by the primitive mind. But nevertheless all those old concepts seem now to be based on heretofore unrecognized factors which relate to a far bigger picture of the universe."

"I *still* need a translation!" insisted the general.

"Even modern technology," confessed the scientist, "has been relatively in a sort of medieval darkness—until now."

"All right," Hart cut in sharply as he glared challengingly at his panel monitors. "You want a real translation? It goes something like this, gentlemen: We've stumbled onto something too big for our britches and we don't dare let go. . . ."

"That's what I'm getting at!" interjected the general adamantly. "The main point is X. We're hanging onto *that*, regardless!"

"The 'regardless' part is the main question," interrupted a council member through monitor 1. "An interesting dilemma. Can a discovery be so great—even in its undeveloped form—that it's worth the risk of extinction?"

"It's extinction now if we *don't* hang onto it!" protested the general heatedly.

"If you're talking about paying the price, Paul," Hart answered, "that's what Jason means by dilemma. This is total commitment for the human race, if you want something to hang your hat on! No holds barred. We found something priceless. Apparently the original proprietors have been around here for ages, a form of super-ultra intelligence we never suspected or conceived of. Now that they know we've got what they want, they're *emerging* . . . !"

"But who or what *are* they?" asked the general in red-faced frustration. "How many? Where? What have they got that we—"

"Plenty!" interrupted Hart. "You know how Kettleridge died. And that's why Dave Duqayne is a sitting duck right now! This is Pandora's box, and we don't dare tell the public about it. We have to meet this crisis on a new international level that must remain invisible—a global echelon that they may *never* know about, from here on in. . . ."

"I see," said MI-7 from Trafalgar Square. "We're talking about a Sixth Estate—a secret government hidden from the world. Hmm. I don't mind telling you, gentlemen, that both the P.M. and the Crown are gravely concerned—"

"Concerned!" exclaimed J.A. incredulously. "Who the hell isn't? We've just hung out the bait and our mysterious quarry is starting to respond. We don't know if we're dealing with demigods or demons. Why else would there be an Omega Condition Three, for God's sake? With *X* we've either stumbled across the Golden Fleece, or it's a direct connection to Hell! Whether for good or evil, gentlemen, the old points of reference are gone—*the lid is off!*"

To David Alexander Duqayne, midnight in a dark
museum was a proper time and place for his ghastly
mood. The loneliness he felt was not the sentimental
kind. It was standing in smouldering desolation unable to scream. It was perceiving a dropped stitch in
some cosmic sampler. Or hearing the gears and axles
of the destiny machine straining to break.

Months before this moment the indefatigable Dr.
Damon Kettleridge lay nobly blank, staringly rigid
and horribly dead on the cold marble slab of a stuffy
British mausoleum, the victim of a sinister event.
The incredible autopsy had no precedent in science.
Now, here in Los Angles, the circumstances leading
to the bizarre murder had been duplicated. Would it
happen again?

If one waited for something to happen and knew
with a congenital instinct that it was *going* to happen
but didn't know when, it left one mentally staring.
To make things worse, if everyone else disbelieved
this dire event that one had predicted, it left one
skewered on the horns of a ridiculous dilemma. *If* it
happened, one could possibly die; and if it did *not*
happen, one's reputation would be rivuleted with egg.
But a terrible urgency drove one to the gamble. One
waited and one stared mentally, impaled on splinters
of borrowed time.

Hidden behind a tall showcase of early Arabic and
Egyptian sand-mold glass, Duqayne was well-camou-
flaged but not physically alone. Brockway's insidious
bulk, including Van Dyke and unlighted briar, was
hunched behind the Etruscan armor only eighteen feet
away, and somewhere beyond were the waiting government men and two armed museum guards. Somewhere else, unpinpointed as usual, Mike Havelin was

scoffing at this special setup and likely to blow the whole trap. But he had to have Mike here. There was no one else he could trust—not any more.

Except for Lillian Hart, he thought, with a pavement-wide trace of libido. As her tall svelte willowy blue-eyed brunette vision came to him, he felt surreptitiously possessive but lonelier than before. Eighteen incredible months on this case, and tonight perhaps the finale. Was he on a dead-end trail or about to open the gates of Hell? Engagements *did* have their limits, but could he marry her if—

"*Ps-s-st! Hey, Dave!*"

The hoarse whisper at his elbow almost made him jump through the showcase. It was Mike Havelin, his square, hand-lined profile barely discernible in the deep gloom. "What the hell!" he whispered back. "Stay put, will you?"

"Who're you kidding, Injun? Ten-to-one you get stood up—no takers."

"Shut up!"

"All those late-late movies. You should try sleeping, or maybe yoga."

"Mike, I'm asking you—"

"Okay, okay. We killed two hours already. Why not try for five?"

"You bring your hardware?"

"Aw come on, daddy!"

"One cliché deserves another—I kid you *not*. . . ."

They waited there together in the vaulted silence, occasionally staring across the aisle at the booby trap. There, under the polished plate glass of a table case was Exhibit 9241-612, by now internationally advertised in the most conservative curator journals and catalogs. The small, geared instrument was artificially age-patinaed and properly dated with radioactive carbon, purported to be a second artefact excavated from the Nieuwald Mine in South Africa. The first and only genuine article, British Museum Exhibit 1247, had invited burglary and murder—also the sober attention of the U.S. Senate Security Com-

13

mittee, and a secret research grant in microbiology and genetics. That's where Dr. Irving Brockway had come in. Now, after long investigation, closed-door committee hearings, security-strangled press conferences and somber bouts with conscience, Duqayne stood poised to wield the sword of Perseus or to go go down in flames.

Yesterday's back-page article in the L.A. papers had finally made a strike: *U.S. Government concern . . . imminent confiscation of Exhibit 9241-612 . . . metallurgical analysis. . . .* Late in the afternoon, a cultured voice on the phone, clinically precise, vastly authoritative, inquiring about the exhibit. Frequency analysis proved it to be coming through an electronic filter. A voice-print would have been useless. That single call was not from a crackpot. It had the gilt-edged label of top-echelon organization.

When Duqayne remembered the classified details of the British Museum murder, he felt very much like tethered bait. The looming darkness was alive with a thousand eyes. And that, he reflected sheepishly, had all the ammoniac impact of five hundred drooling tigers.

Somewhere distantly in the catacombs of the museum, a telephone started to ring. "Damn!" said Duqayne aloud.

"The guard will get it," advised Brockway from his pit of darkness. "Stay put, Dave!"

"A phone call?" muttered Mike suspiciously. "Here? At this time of night?"

"Relax," Duqayne told him. "All trunks are tied to the tape circuits. If it's anything, we can play it back."

"That's nasty."

"I learned it from *you.*"

"And a lot more, buddy. Remember that."

"Yeah. With the scars to prove it!"

They both fell silent, inevitably recalling their commando days. Mike had been his combat instructor.

A flashlight glimmered. It was one of the museum

guards. "There's a call for Captain Wishnow," he announced, his voice echo-chambered by the acoustics of the exhibit hall.

"Great!" Mike chuckled derisively. "Maybe his girl friend stood him up—tired of waiting."

Brockway loomed upon them, lighting his pipe. "Might as well take five," he said.

"Brock?"

"Yes, Dave?"

"Are your ears ringing?"

"What?"

"I said are your ears ringing?"

"No."

All three turned briefly to watch Captain Wishnow's silhouette pass through the dimly lighted doorway at the end of the vast room.

"You trying to tell us something?" asked Mike.

Duqayne ignored the question. "Where's Wishnow's sidekick—what'shisname?"

"Lieutenant Bass," replied Brockway. "He's still up there in the mummy section. Why?"

"I don't know. I'm turning on the lights."

"Not yet, Dave." Irv Brockway's barrel-chested voice was always irritatingly calm. "Lights would be seen from the street."

"All right, but I'm goin, to check around."

"Dave—" Mike started to protest but then remembered their signals. They had talked about Brockway in private. Mike hadn't worked on the case until now. Duqayne wanted his personal impression of the inscrutable microbiologist.

"Be back in a minute," Dave said, and left the two alone together.

As he moved up the aisle toward the corridor entrance, Dave flashed the thin beam of his penlight across the tiled floor. There *had* been a faint ringing in his ears, which he had sensed twice before under peculiar circumstances, and this time he liked it even less. Objectively, he wondered if he were an idiot gone soft in the head; but subjectively, his presentiment of alien instrumentality sent worms of goose-flesh slithering over his back. And who could you tell a thing like *that* to? He had aired his suspicions once to Brockway right in the middle of the K-chromosome research and had been academically squelched.

If somebody *really* sharp were going to lift that exhibit he certainly wouldn't blunder into this trap like a second-storey mechanic. Whatever was going to happen was going to occur with surprising finesse—if it wasn't happening already!

His flashlight beam stopped on a broad white square of tile. It was against the wall in the area where Wishnow had been concealed. Glittering back at him was a ruby-red, dollar-sized spat of fresh blood.

The lights went on in the museum hall and Captain Wishnow stood at the door staring at him. He was a tall man in his mid-thirties, well built, prematurely balding, with the tanned leathery look of a football coach combined with the slight tweediness of an upper-echelon government agent. Wishnow knew what Duqayne had discovered. He approached leisurely with a friendly grin. "Watch out for that Persian bronze stuff," he said. "I lost some skin on it." With a handkerchief he wiped a trickle of blood from his forehead.

"What's with the lights?" asked Duqayne, unsmiling. The ringing in his ears was back again.

Wishnow shrugged. "That was a call from HQ. There's been a change in plans."

By now, Lieutenant Bass, Brockway, and Havelin were joining them. "What kind of a change?" asked Brockway.

"They want the exhibit. That's all I can tell you." "Johnson, do you have the key to that case?"

"Yes, sir, but—"

"Good. Let's have it."

As the guard moved toward them, Duqayne took a quick survey of the others present. The distant ringing, more in his brain than in his ears, seemed to affect his vision. He saw them all as though through a filter; they were surrealistic. Especially young Lieutenant Bass, looking pale, semi-rigid, as though coming out of a trance. Brockway was bigger than life, embracing the scene more than dominating it with his powerful presence. Mike Havelin, crew-cut and hard-jawed, locked questioning eyes on Dave, probing for a signal.

"Brock—maybe I'd better check the tapes on that call."

Brockway shrugged deceptively obese shoulders. "If it'll make you feel better, Dave."

"Forget it," said Wishnow. "I had to destroy them."

Brockway narrowed beady black eyes. "You destroyed the recording tapes? Why?"

"This thing is Top Secret, so as far as you're concerned, Dr. Brockway—"

"As far as I'm concerned," boomed Brockway, "I'm still in charge of this project." He moved quickly, appropriating the key from the guard. "I'll have to make a phone call, myself, before I'll permit the exhibit to be removed."

"Sorry, Doctor." Wishnow smiled at him. "You're in charge of the project's scientific aspects, *not* the security." He held out his hand. "The key, please."

On an irrepressible impulse, Duqayne stepped between the two men and looked closely at Wishnow. "You know, I hate to tell you this," he said coldly, "but your slip is showing. That blood on the floor—" He pointed at it. "It's not yours, Buster, *whoever* you are!"

He had a very fleeting impression of Mike and Brockway reacting to the blood-spot discovery, but his main preoccupation was with Wishnow. The mental ringing revved up hard, distorting his vision. He only dimly remembered leaping forward, yelling out an unknown primordial hate and tearing at the man's face with his fingernails. There was other swift movement, perhaps a gunshot. His mind was seared by a tidal flame-wave that was shadow-paced by a vision out of Hell—a foto-scar that he would never erase. Then he chuted the flood into a widening abyss of darkness. . . .

∞

She was a fairly tall brunette, twenty-six years old, and otherwise about 34-24-35—lithe, gently suntanned, and just now noticeably two-toned due to a total absence of bikini. The way she held that proud head on her very female shoulders was both patrician and pagan; especially the latter, with her dark hair let down halfway to her naked waist, and with the low-key bedlamp making soft twin crescents of her breasts as she smiled at him.

"Hello," he said, wondering that he was still alive.

She sighed out his name and came into the bed with him then, and he took the long smooth softness of her hungrily into his arms. "Mike called me from the receiving hospital and I brought you home," she told him. "You poor, dumb, stubborn angel—when are you ever going to give up this bogeyman carnival of yours!"

He stopped kissing her and got up on an elbow to peer at his surroundings. *"Home?"* he queried. The knotty pine walls and functional furnishings were not what one would expect of a Hart mansion bedroom.

"Not in town, silly—we're down at the beach!"

The cabalistic decorations and the voodoo masks should have told him as much. She was a nut on astrology and the occult—maybe a neophyte sorceress. A young one with the demon fires in her, judging by the way she burned in his arms.

"And besides, you know Dad's never waved a shot-gun at you."

"That's because I haven't gotten you pregnant."

"I've never given you a fighting chance, but if this engagement stretches out any longer, my failsafe is going to blow a fuse!"

"Lillian, honey, I'm sorry to talk shop at a time like this, but—" He looked around for a phone and she pressed melony softness against him, pouting.

18

"Oh all right, so I'll give you a report. They were worried about you there for a while. You had some kind of a fit, according to Dr. Brockway. My little poltergeists keep telling me not to like that man. He looks like he swallowed a Maltese Falcon."

"Lil—what did they do with Wishnow?"

"Oh he was all right—just a few scratches. . . ."

Duqayne braced himself tensely on both elbows and stared into space. He was back in that smouldering desolation unable to scream, unable to tell even *her*. Maddeningly, he could vividly reconstruct the whole masquerade. Wishnow, calmly solicitous: *Your boy has a problem, Brockway. I'd look into that before you go on with the project* . . . And Brockway as frustratingly enigmatic as ever: *I'll do that, Captain— maybe he's been working too hard. Don't know what came over him. . . .*

"Lil—what about Mike?"

"He seemed more worried about you than anybody, and no wonder! Do you know what you had him doing? Cleaning your fingernails!"

"Fingernails!" Duqayne quickly examined his nails. "Where did he do it?"

"Don't worry, your reputation is still salvageable. Nobody saw him except me. You kept yelling that you were contaminated."

"Okay, okay, but *then* what?"

"He said to be sure to tell you that a Dr. Chafey would have your prescription ready in the morning, whatever *that* is."

Duqayne collapsed back onto the pillow. "Thank God!" He closed his eyes in relief. Their signals had worked all the way. Good old Mike—always in there when you needed him! Suddenly, his eyes snapped open and he stared up into Lillian Hart's loving blue eyes. "Mike? He knows we're here together?"

"He helped me bring you here. You could hardly drive under sedation, darling. The doctor at the receiving hospital said you'd be all right."

"To hell with the doctor—I'm thinking of Mike!"

She kissed his nose gently. "Now when are we going to settle all that? So we all grew up together and our puppy-love was as three-cornered as a didey. But there comes a time, sweetie—"

"Yeah." He held her to him and brushed his lips against her shoulder, still remembering.

"Now David—if *I* can make the adjustment—"

"I know, I know, but I don't take such a kindly fate for granted. When I think of Mike now, I say there but for the grace of God—"

"Shush!"

"You know what I mean. It might have turned out the other way after our baby-fat years. If *he* were here tonight instead of me—or any other night—I know the kind of hell I'd be going through."

"Mike loves us both like a brother. He's very happy for us."

"Oh sure! Schizo-happy. Well, life's bigger than all of us. . . ."

"So mote it be!"

"Look, witch—cast me no spells tonight!"

"Why *not?*" There was a happy wickedness in her eyes.

He kissed her, and there was devilishly more. And for a long, long while there was no further conversation. Nor any more ringing in his ears—not just now. . . .

∞

The malefic gargoyle thing was a hell-face in black ebony, looming upon him with a carnivorous sneer. It matched the dreams he had emerged from. One of Lillian's imported demon masks hung on the wall over a runic sign she had wrought on parchment in ritualistic black paint:

ᘓ ᘔ ᖿ ᖆ ᕯ ᘞ
ᖆ ᘘ ᘚ ᘓ ᘓ

There was an evil to the runes, something in their unknown meaning that jangled discordantly like a banshee wail echoing mournfully in the dark caverns of the atavistic and subliminal. He experienced mental revulsion. Damn!

He turned to wake her up, but the bed beside him was empty. He lay in running rivulets of sweat, aware of a siege of nightmares. His face felt scratched and torn and caked with blood. What in grisly hell had happened? He stumbled out of bed and found the bathroom, a functional knotty pine water closet with toilet and washbowl and a curtained shower compartment.

When he got to the medicine cabinet mirror, his swarthy countenance stared back at an unscarred face. A Quichuan-Spanish ancestor had reached through his mixed French-Irish origins to give him the prominent nose, full lips, high cheekbones, and mahogany complexion of the Bolivian Alto Plano—one of the sources of Mike's nickname of "Injun." Though somewhat craggy-jawed and shaggy-browed, his brooding visage bore no sign of blood or scratches. He had dreamed it—those thousand eyes in the night, and a ringing crescendo in his brain that was a scream of demons clawing at him in the suffocating dark of an infinite tomb.

He supported himself with both hands on the washbowl, his head bending down in agony. *"Why,* for the love of God!" Why was *he* singled out for this special knowledge of the damned? He should have dropped the whole case before it started. Now even Lillian—

From his lowered angle of vision he could see under the bed. Lillian's night bag was still there. A flood of relief washed over him and he straightened up slowly. She hadn't left him! In the mirror he noticed the shower curtain rod behind him decorated with her beige stockings and her small sheer white step-ins. Beside him were three new guest towels on a rack. They were embroidered successively with the captions: His, Hers, and Intruders. He knew this was

21

good for a grin, but there wasn't any in him. He returned to the bedroom to put on his pants and shirt.

There was a long moment in which he sat on the edge of the bed and contemplated the subject of Lillian Hart. Due to no fault of their own, their love affair was booby-trapped. Aside from his present involvement with a detective case that had gone G-2, and was sucking him into weirdsville, there was the awesome spectre of her father. Not a damn thing wrong with good old John Anthony Hart—a man among men and a fighter—but he was terribly contaminated with money. Through the years, Duqayne had seen this distortion coming, and so had Mike Havelin, with equal misgivings. Marrying the daughter of a successful businessman, or maybe even a millionaire, was one thing, but the daughter of J.A. Hart was quite another. When an ordinary Joe Shmo marries into more than a *billion* dollars, he acquires an immediate stigma of gigolo—or at least the royal consort—and instantly starts life in a fishbowl.

Already the offer was there for him, a fat vice-presidency in one of forty-eight Hart International divisions—or was it fifty-two this year? The whole organization was a self-propagating conglomerate mutual fund. He loved the kaleidoscopic pixy named Lil; he had grown up with her before Hart had moved to Success Street; but the dowry angle was a bad scene for an ex-G.I. commando and intelligence agent who, at least until recently, had helped his war-buddy operate a middle-class private detective agency.

After last night, who could guess the crumble of the cookie? A premonition had begun to haunt him that he was no longer his own master, that he was becoming some kind of pawn on a cosmic chessboard. But Lillian was an innocent bystander, and in a vague apprehensive sort of way he had even started to consider protecting her from himself.

Then again he had several times rejected this as depressive and had forced himself to think of wedding bells. But today wasn't one of those days. He went to the beach side of the cottage and peered outside just as a distant freighter blew its fog horn. The low overcast sky suffused the early daylight, bleeding color out of the mournful sea . . . and the grayness of the world reached from his sacroiliac all the way to God. . . .

∞

A short time later he saw her lonely figure on the two-mile stretch of private beach. The property was a Hart International acquisition for one of the hotel divisions. As a matter of fact, the main beach house was a sprawling, fully-staffed mansion on the nearby peninsula, largely reserved for Hart's numerous traveling executives and/or their V.I.P. clients. But Lillian preferred the knotty pine guest cottage for her own brand of proprietary isolation. Nothing had orphaned her more than her father's money.

She wore yellow slacks and a matching turtleneck. Her feet were bare and the dark cornucopia of her hair was swept back into a gossamer snood. She looked up at him sadly but without reproach. He sat down beside her and just stared out wordlessly at the flat kelp beds of the morning low tide, listening to the rusty-tackle screeching of the gulls.

After a sensible interlude, she took his hand and pressed it to her cheek. That was Lillian, he thought. Ten thousand words in a gesture.

"Are you hungry?" she said. 'There's some country sausage. . . . Eggs and coffee of course."

"I've got to make some phone calls."

"Dr. Chafey?"

"Yes. And Brock and I have that thing to go through at the college this afternoon."

"I read about it."

"It's a combination student conference and a last meeting with the press."

"*Last* meeting?"

"That was our agreement. If last night's museum

caper didn't catch me a bogeyman I was to throw in the towel. In fact, it's practically a government ultimatum."

Lillian began to study him hopefully. "That explains Senator Cain maybe?"

"Yeah. He's the Security Committee tie-in to the whole project. He'll be there to shoot me down publicly, I guess, if I make any more waves."

"Like those articles you wrote about the Kettleridge papers before the government closed the lid."

"I was out of my mind to get involved with the exploiters—Sunday supplements, no less. Now I'm like a flying saucer buff who has to be the whipping boy to get the powers-that-be off a hot spot."

She sighed deeply. "Well—that retires the insidious Dr. Brockway, and now I presume I've acquired a prospective husband?" As he only stared fixedly at the sea, the silence grew sticky. "Don't force me to hex up a love philter, sweetie. I'm fresh out of periwinkle and bergamot."

So this was the day she had picked for a showdown after these months of waiting. Not to answer a chin-out naked question like that from your love-mate was brutal, he knew, but he couldn't look at her when he thought of his still unfinished, still very deadly business—a race against time before that campus confab. There was Dr. Chafey, the last thin thread that could tie him like a fly to a monstrous web—one that could make him a prisoner forever. Or free him once and for all.

Suddenly, Lillian scrambled to her feet and walked away from him. He watched her go—a warm and vibrant young Eve as rich as an empress, a hip modern beauty who should have given the regal nod by now to any one of a dozen platinum-heeled international playboys who had chased her in great bewilderment from Hollywood to Cannes and Zurich, and from Athens to Beirut and Hong Kong. They had ultimately shrugged her off as a female nut who apparently had her own private Yoga-cult or other

24

form of hallucinogenics. To them she was a riddle, but to Dave Duqayne and Mike Havelin, she was a pigtailed tomboy on a raft in childhood's mystic noon of long ago—also a miracle of sudden womanhood when they returned from the war.

Brilliant, educated to boredom, she had waited quietly for love and found it to be complicated by their competitive devotion. While waiting for them to break up their own impasse, she had gone existentialist, esoteric, Zen, Hindu—the total avant-garde gamut including the occult. He and Mike had taken it with a grain of salt. They knew she was too earthy to be bent out of shape by abstractions; also too rugged for any such narcissistic foibles as self-pity, paranoia, or masochism—as evidenced by her lack of any serious commitment to the cap-and-acid scene. Astrology had fascinated her as a research lark; whereas the witchcraft was a game—a mood toy, a pallet of quixotic colorations, a charade with many masks to cover the unchangeable in her. She merely longed for the simplicity of being, and an uncomplicated love.

But from where *he* sat and from where *she* sat, a simple wish like that was a great big grimy brass key to Hell. In fact it was a never-ending source of wonder to him why she didn't tell him to go there.

He finally went after her and found her staring at sand crabs among the barnacled rocks and tide pools. As he had expected, it was too much for human nature not to trigger an emotional crisis—the cold shoulder and tears and the stomping and shouting, not unmixed with some fairly ballistic missiles aimed at his masculine vanity.

To sum it up, he could go dreck in his hat. Who the hell did he think he was to tear somebody apart like this, not letting her share with him what was driving him batty? Last night he had screamed like a drunk with the D.T.'s or a mainliner without a fix. She had slapped him, fought him, called him everything she could think of, and finally had fled from him to save herself from being strangled.

"Baby, I'm sorry," he said. "I should stay away from you for your own good. I can't help it if—"

"The hell you can't! I love you, dammit, and if you loved *me* you'd see a headshrinker! Don't worry about the bill—I'll buy you a university full of them if that's what it takes!"

When he glared at her she softened. "Darling, forgive me, but you just can't exclude me from what happens to you!"

"I'm trying to—it can get still rougher."

"But you said that today at the college would be the wrap-up of the whole mess!"

"Maybe, honey, maybe. What got out to the public is one thing—we're deliberately giving it the screwball angle, and I'm the goat. But what's classified in this case is strictly another matter. You don't know what's involved."

"Of course I do—don't hand me that! I'm under the same roof with Dad, you know. He's *had* to clear me with security. I've followed every bit of the Kettleridge case from the beginning."

"Oh? That's very interesting. Why don't you tell me what you know?"

"Don't be ridiculous. It's too long a story."

"Maybe this much I *do* owe you, Lil. I can fill in the details that few people know about—and maybe a few that Brockway hasn't heard of."

She studied him carefully. "All right, David," she said, slowly. "Go ahead."

"No, I mean you tell *me* what you know and I'll fill in the carefully premeditated gaps."

She hesitated, then smiled. "Well, that sounds like a fair proposition."

"There's a string attached."

"What is it?"

"Your promise never to reveal to *anyone* what I tell you—except maybe Mike, if it's absolutely need-to-know."

"Oh wow!"

"Take it or leave it!"

"Come on!" She took his hand. "Let's fire up those sausages!"

"Lil!"

"Oh all right—I promise!"

"That had better be more than a Campfire Girl's honor."

In a precarious silence they walked back to the cottage, but at the front steps she seemed to murmur aloud to herself. "It's one side of the witch's pyramid."

"*What* is?"

"Secrecy."

"And the other three sides?"

She opened the door and waved him inside with a laconic smirk. "That's a secret."

Incongruously over a cheerful spread of sausage and eggs, they reviewed the macabre details of the Kettleridge case together, Lillian rather flippantly leading with what she had read or gotten from her father or Mike, and Duqayne interrupting occasionally to add the missing pieces.

Publicly it was known that the late Dr. Damon Kettleridge had been a highly respected biochemist for one of Hart International's research foundations. Not so public was the fact that he had been a close personal friend of J.A. Hart, as well as a geologist and an archaeologist. His apparently unsolvable murder had led to a personal contract from Hart with Havelin-Duqayne Associates for a private investigation. Mike had been tied up on an embezzlement case, so Duqayne had picked up the Kettleridge mystery alone. It was when he tied the bizarre autopsy to Kettleridge's biochemical research, and his archaeological theories, that the U.S. Government and Dr. Brockway had come into the picture.

"So now the government wants out," said Lillian. "What turned them off?"

"Brockway. His experiments seemed to disprove Kettleridge's claims."

"Just who *is* Dr. Brockway? Where did they dig him up from?"

"You're getting ahead of the story. Now you say you know about Kettleridge's archaeological hobby and his pet theory about the origin of Man."

"It's nothing new. Romantic amateurs have often come up with the same idea for ages, attempting to tie ancient legends to it, such as the battle of the

Titans, the Thunderbolt of Zeus, the Eye of Odin. . . ."

"Exactly—get it? Titans: giants or supermen. Thunderbolt: atom bomb, laser, death ray. And that last one gives a hint of pre-diluvian television, or maybe a stationary satellite. That's the basic idea."

Lillian sighed. "Here we go with Daeniken and 'Chariots of the Gods.' Maybe you should join the Ancient Astronauts."

"It's something like that but much bigger—a more ancient and complex picture. But one basic factor lies behind both the Daeniken and Kettleridge theories: long before our so-called written history, in the *real* dawn of time, some of our mixed ancestors are supposed to have come from the stars."

"And Kettleridge believes their strain is still carried in modern man. . . ."

"In *some* men, yes. He bases it on the theory of the K-chromosome, plus a rare antibody found in rare samples of Rh-negative blood. Somebody did research once on the remains of a weird humanoid creature discovered in Canada. Wolves had made a fresh kill and the cell and blood structure was still good enough for analysis. There've been a few other such cases, and Kettleridge made a specialty of the study. He concluded that the strain is something like a 'missing link'—but *upward* on the evolutionary scale, not downward. Apparently, the rare blood antigen involved is supposed to give almost total immunity to disease. The Canadian snow creature was some kind of hybrid degeneration; but the *true* strain, according to his theory, may be around today in limited numbers—and *not* degenerated. In fact—"

"Sounds kind of flimsy, David."

"Not necessarily. After all, chromosome research has only recently come into a high state of the art. There hasn't been time yet to make a representative scan of chromosome types. In fact, recognition of the X-double-Y chromosome in insanity cases has only come up in the past few years. So why shouldn't the K-type have remained hidden?"

"How did Brockway disprove Kettleridge's findings?"

"He didn't."

"But you said—"

"I said the government seems to accept it. I don't. In fact I think it's a coverup—they're holding the lid on something."

"But what was his proof?"

"He set up a skimpy so-called international program and finally sampled only a few thousand blood-bank donations from all parts of the world, strictly Rh-negatives, of course. No super-antigens. Kettleridge called the rare blood Rh-U. There was no sign of it."

"Well, that's fairly conclusive, isn't it?"

"But he didn't go into chromosomes at all, and as for blood—any Rh-U type isn't about to donate a blood sample if he can help it!"

"David, I read your article based on the Kettleridge papers."

"And?"

"Your whole idea is that people with K-chromosomes carry the genes of the original star people."

"And?"

"According to you and Kettleridge, such people are way-out mental mutations. Oh Dave—how did you ever fall for a comic-book notion like that?"

"The government didn't think it was so comical there for a while. Parapsychology has emerged from the comic books—you should certainly know that with *your* hobbies! And mental mutations could conceivably impersonate some very important people, such as representatives to peace conferences and the like."

"What ever turned the government on in the first place? I mean what specific fact?"

"There were a number of puzzle pieces that suddenly came together, and they didn't spell Mother. One was the British Museum exhibit that somebody robbed, which was Kettleridge's motivation for going to London. He insisted on tracing it down."

"Wait a minute!" Lillian protested in sudden

puzzlement. "If somebody *took* the exhibit from the British Museum, they got what they wanted, didn't they? So why should they rise to the bait you set out for them here in Los Angeles?"

Duqayne frowned at her but with the trace of a grim smile. "Now you're getting to the rips in the fabric, Lil. You're right—why should 'they,' as you call them, be interested in something they've already got? It's at this point where the *double* play comes in. Somebody knows something they're not telling—I mean on *our* side. Don't ask me who. I've had a personal theory that before the British Museum gizmo was ever put on display, it had *something* taken out of it—and it's that 'something' that the baddies are still desperately trying to locate."

"What gave you that idea?"

"I don't know—maybe my Indian spirit guide, or as Mike puts it, too many late-late movies. But the proof of it came when all the top brass bought my plan. Your ever-loving papa wouldn't have gone for it if there wasn't more to the picture than appears on the surface, and certainly Brockway—"

"David, I'm not following you. If they know someting that important, why shouldn't they—"

"Tell me?" He broke in with a tight-lipped smirk. "Honey, I'm telling you this is bigger and more complex than your garden variety fantasies. I think something's been discovered—*inside* of the original contraption—that's caught the world with its pants down. It's too big or too dangerous to talk about. So when I cooked up this idea of putting a duplicate gizmo on display—and when nobody stopped me—it meant that the unseen opposition was still looking for their long-lost marbles. They had to figure that more was found originally than they had expected. They evidently couldn't take chances, so they came to have a look."

"Dave, that's *your* theory. How do you know that anything unusual happened last night? It may have been nothing but that hyped-up imagination of yours. It seems to be in high gear."

"I'll know more about that when I hear from Mike or Dr. Chafey."

There was a brief pause while they stared at each other searchingly over their coffee. Finally, Lillian sighed with evident dissatisfaction. "I know about the British contraption, as you call it. It was brought from that mine in South Africa."

"Cut out of a limestone grotto at the 8,000-foot level—a geological formation proven to be over *50,000 years old*—imperishable metal, and fossil footprints. Not bare feet, but oversized *sandals*. Those ancients were about eight feet tall. They lived underground to escape the cataclysm of the so-called Deluge."

Lillian put down her coffee and made an impatient gesture of rejection. "Come *on*, sweetie! The rankest amateur sci-fi fan and convention follower can quote you chapter and verse on all that! We've all been there—Charles Fort, Shaver, Daeniken. . . . Any of them could finish the plot. You claimed in your article that these ancient super-beings don't want to be discovered, and that's why they absconded with the British Museum exhibit—also, when Kettleridge got too hot on their trail, they killed him."

"We were talking about the *government*, Lil. We've only covered one of several pieces of the puzzle. The next one was the autopsy. Kettleridge's brain was burned out—dendrites singed back and synapses widened as though a short circuit had hit every neuron in his head."

"So? He was electrocuted."

"No electric shock victim has any record of such an autopsy. It's never happened before. The government feared a new kind of weapon."

"But *you* infer that Kettleridge was killed by a *mental* force."

"Yup. An ESP power that comes close to godliness —and that, baby, is not funny!" Duqayne had been pacing the floor, and now he paused at a bookcase to search through its occult-dominated contents.

Lillian began to worry at him. "David, honey—you *can't* believe all that!"

Dave pointed to her books. "Look who's talking!" He picked out a few samples—riffled their pages. "'Psychic Experiences' . . . 'Mastering Witchcraft' . . . 'Vampires in Europe' . . . 'Black Magic and Cults' . . . 'Cosmic Mysteries of the Universe'. . . ." He raised a quizzical brow at her. "Baby, you don't seem to have a priority on the phlegmatic view."

"Dave," she countered, with just a tinge of frustration, "we're talking about *you*—not fantasy."

"Okay." He walked back to the breakfast table with a copy of the Presbyterian Bible. "I'll give you the scariest one of them all. Do you call *this* fantasy?" She stared at it as he placed it in front of her. "Witches are supposed to know all about the antiquities."

"I am *not* a witch!" she said, with fervent emphasis. Then, controlling herself, she placed a gentle hand on the Bible. "And for this very reason." Her voice lowered; her gaze was beyond him. "Witchcraft takes a certain—commitment."

"What—blasphemy?"

"In a sense . . . maybe it's a matter of opinion."

"But you believe the Bible."

"Yes."

"Fine! Then just for kicks, open it and read me Genesis six, verse four."

"Oh for—! David, every witch or neophyte in the occult knows that verse by heart!"

"Do they?" He glared at her with a challenging intentness. "Read it anyway."

She opened the well-worn book and found the place. Almost wearily, she sighed out the familiar words. *"There were giants in the earth in those days—"*

"Curious preposition there," he interrupted. "Not *on* the earth, but *in* the earth. Do you know the Catholics got to that one and changed it to *upon* the earth?"

Her troubled gaze parted from his reluctantly, and she read further. "—*And also after that when the sons of God came in unto the daughters of men—*"

"No immaculate conception there! Or would you believe—*mental* parthenogenesis?"

"Shush! —*and they bare children to them, the same became mighty men—*' "

"Mutants."

"—*Which were of old, men of renown.*"

As she looked up at him in some apprehension, he elaborated. "One of the most mysterious passages of the Bible, that. God knows what else may have been burned in the libraries of Alexandria. You know, some kind of a wrestling match has been going on between scholars and priests and translators through the ages on that little verse—as though *some* people wanted to garble it up deliberately."

"Aren't you rationalizing?"

"Not particularly when I've gotten some expert input on the original translations. The giants were known in the old books as the Nephilim—it's all there, millenia before Christ. And note that a distinction is made between the 'giants' and the 'sons of God.' Kettleridge believed there were two breeds of extraterrestrial visitors: good and evil. I could add to that. I think maybe there were also some retrogressive freaks—the Puget Sound Indians, the Abominable Snowman, and other versions. But the *real* boys to watch out for are the straight-line K-chromosome carriers. These are dangerous mental mutations. I think they've had a lot to do with the history *and* some of the voodoo and witchcraft of this poor old rocky world."

Lillian got up abruptly from the table. "*Will* you stop it!" When he stared at her in sudden puzzlement, she opened up on him. "You're all worked up about that old ghost story as though you'd discovered it all by yourself!"

"I suppose you know *more?*"

"Of course I do! I can quote you the Book of Noah

and trace the remnants of your monster people, clear into England and the Druids if you want. Actually, you're talking about one of the basic catachisms of witchcraft itself, but it doesn't prove anything. I can give you the whole bit, from the fall of Shathanus, or Azael, clear through the Retaliation—"

"You mean, the Deluge."

"Yes, and to all the legends beyond—of their survival after Atlantis. The Titans and all the rest. Out of the fragments of their knowledge, sorcery and alchemy were supposed to have been derived. . . ."

"Lil, you're a paradoxical pixy, do you know it? You wade through miles of esoteric stuff—all freaked out into the Big Blue—and then suddenly you turn square. No take."

"What do you want me to do, conjure up an elemental?"

"You're dodging something. I don't think you're consciously the devious type, so your subconscious must be working overtime with its defense mechanisms."

"Don't sell me *that!*"

"Then will you admit that all these esoterica and biblical inputs tend to draw a definite pattern?"

"What kind of pattern?"

"One that points to the existence of an ancient pool of knowledge, of such proportions that it *had* to be imported?"

"Maybe it's universal wishful thinking. We all have the Messianic complex."

"Come on, Lil—you said that the survivors of this ancient super-race entered into Europe. Even in *Beowulf*—"

"The Sword of Hrothgar? I can quote *that* inscription, too! 'The story of ancient wars between good and evil, the Flood sweeping the Giants away, how they suffered and died, that race who hated the Ruler of us all.' " She paused, watching his reaction. "Shall I go on?"

"Yes, Lil. Tell me more."

She turned away and walked to the window. He followed her.

"David, what I'm trying to say is that myths are myths, and today is today. You *can't* let such fantasy enter your life!" Since he only studied her in silence, she finally asked, "What does the government say about Genesis 6:4?"

"The Bible isn't up their legal alley. They'd have to consider it irrelevant—also irreverent, to please the voters. But there *are* a couple of puzzle pieces I've kept to myself."

"Such as?"

"Well, for one thing—I'm a target."

She turned, her blue eyes widening at him. "For whom?"

He shrugged. "*You* name them. What are they? Nephilim? Overlords? The Unsuspected? I don't know."

Her face was drawn and pale as she looked at him. David, please! I want you to see a psychiatrist; for my sake, if you don't consider yourself. You're very sick!"

His heavy brows lowered at her. "Don't hand me *that* crap, luv! I've had it up to here from Brockway already. He'd *love* to see me on the funny farm. So would Uncle Sam. But I'm *not* crazy—not yet, anyway."

"Darling, you've got to have help!"

"Help? Who's going to give it to me—you and your daddy and your billion bucks? Fat chance!" She started to cry. "Look, baby, you wanted me to spill my guts. Maybe I'd better finish it. You want it all? Every time those bogeymen come near me I get a ringing signal—maybe I'm a borderline sensitive, I don't know. Nobody ever has explained ringing in the ears. It happened to me once in London, once in Washington, and again last night at the museum."

This statement shocked her out of her tears.

"That's right. Your nice normal Captain Wishnow. Brockway said I had a fit, did he? Hell, when I

36

called Wishnow's bluff he almost burned my brain like Kettleridge—that's where those nightmares came from. I *saw* him, Lil. Don't ever ask me to describe it!"

She shrank back slowly from him, instinctively, as though thinking to exorcise an evil presence. "It can't be true—there has to be another explanation."

"Oh, there's an explanation all right. Why did you think I scratched hell out of his face instead of giving him the bum's rush? I told Mike I might do something like that and he thought I was nuts, but when it happened he was set for it."

"Your fingernails!"

"You damn betcha! Who do you suppose Dr. Chafey is? He's Kettleridge's disciple, an authority on all of his work and the one who helped me do that damned article. If *he* finds that skin and blood from my fingernails carries the K-chromosome and Rh-U, then the real Captain Wishnow is a corpse—and you know *what* is a walking fungus-among-us!"

Lillian went back to the table and sat down. He joined her and they sat in a bog of silence. After a while he discovered her studying him with a fearful intensity.

"Dave, I was trying to put myself in your place, believing what you do."

"Smart girl. Maybe you've figured the next step. What if Chafey proves I'm right?"

"I don't give a damn about your mental monsters, true or false—it's *you* who concerns me!"

"What do you expect me to do if I have the positive knowledge that human society has been a chessboard in the hands of these unsuspected mutations for countless ages—just whistle Dixie and take up tiddledywinks?"

"Assuming that you're right—and I can't consciously accept such a horrible concept—but assuming you're right, how could you hope to do anything about it? You say you're a target—why?"

"Obvious. They know that I *know*. That's all."

"But if Chafey's findings are negative, then what?"

The phone rang.

Both of them jumped so severely that it forced an involuntary smile. Duqayne's smile faded first. When she started to answer, he stopped her. "I'll take that." He picked up the receiver and spoke in Spanish. *"Diga?"*

Mike was on the line, speaking hurriedly and low. "You got your proof, baby, but it's secondhand."

"Qué dice, señor?" This "wrong number" bit was an identity signal and a part of their standard tool kit for blocking a line trace in case they were tapped, and Lillian Hart was one trace he never wanted to give the opposition.

"Can it, Gonzales. This is a booth. We're clear."

"You hope! What happened?"

"No answer from your friend this morning, So I went to his lab."

Dave didn't reply immediately, but finally he said, "I can see it now."

"Blown to hell. Homicide's picking up the pieces."

"Do we still have a private file, or is *that* up in smoke?"

"No sweat. We're not connected. Recluse chemist mixes one too many, et cetera. . . ."

"I see. Anything else?"

"Yeah. Like, when you get a chance, Injun, you'd better brief me. Maybe I wasn't listening the first time."

"Are you convinced?"

"I'm convinced that somebody is playing for keeps, whatever the hell this game is all about. And they're no sand-lot club, either, so don't steal any bases until we've had a huddle."

"Do tell."

"Okay. See you on campus. You're making that confab, I suppose?"

"Wouldn't miss it for the world."

"Sorry about your chemical friend, but you two must have known the odds."

"Yeah, thanks—see you."

When he hung up the receiver, Lillian's eyes pleaded. "That was Mike, wasn't it?"

"Yes, Lillian, that was Mike." Duqayne ran a hand through his thick mane of hair to hide the fact that it was trembling slightly. He produced a cigarette. Dave walked to the window and lit up, pulling the smoke in deeply and thinking of the late, faithful Dr. Chafey. Victim number n—an unknown quantity. And who would be next?

Lillian followed him. "Aren't you going to tell me anything?"

He exhaled, then looked at her with new interest. "Yes, lover. I'm going to tell you three things. First of all, I love you." He kissed her half-parted lips. "Second, I've just dropped the Kettleridge case. It's closed."

"David!"

He kissed her again. "And third—you've just trapped yourself a husband."

∞

Like a bomb bursting, the high double doors opened abruptly to release the student assembly. The last speeches had been given, the demands and threats and cross-accusations had been subdued, and all but the sensationalists seemed to be satisfied. Lillian and Mike came out ahead òf the avalanche, and he wore a wistful grin as he discovered a tear in her eye. "It's over, Lil. I actually think he means it. He's through with the case."

"I won't believe it until he walks out of there!"

"Only a few more minutes, honey, then all you two will have to think about is wedding bells."

"Mike, I'm sorry about everything being on such short notice, but—"

"I know. Good old Hart International just happened to have a private plane available for Acapulco next week. Don't kid your Uncle Michael, baby, you've had plan X set up and waiting for our boy for a long time. You're not fooling me!"

She smiled at him gratefully. "Yes I have, Mike. For years!"

"Oh now I wouldn't drag it back *that* far. Nature will out, and all that, but I like to remember the times when I still had you guessing."

"You're sweet."

"I'm a mangey mongrel and I bite!"

"But you won't let us down, will you?"

He patted her hand where it rested on his arm. "I wouldn't miss the irony of it for the world. Why do they call the guy that loses the best man? He's the one that's supposed to win!"

Behind them, students, faculty members and visitors made way for a slow-moving wedge of commotion. Newsmen still crowded in to get flash photos of Duqayne, flanked by Senator Cain and Dr. Brockway. There were handshakes and tag-ends of oratory, praising the senator, praising Brockway's contributions, and also praising Duqayne for taking a realistic stand.

"What do you say to that, Senator?" asked a reporter. "He really shut them up in there today, didn't he?"

Senator Cain was tall, bareheaded, in his lean fifties; blond-haired, blue-eyed, commanding. He smiled thinly. "If he hadn't shut them up, the government would have had to do it *for* him."

As reporters pressed Duqayne, himself, for a statement, Brockway warded them off. "I'm sorry, boys, this thing is all wrapped up. The investigation is closed. . . ."

Duqayne seemed wryly amused. "Don't you think I can handle it, Brock? It's over, isn't it?" But he *wasn't* amused, and it *wasn't* over. The smouldering desolation was back and the screaming with no one to hear. Had he been mad to risk everything on one desperate camouflage? Distantly, again there was a sense of ringing, an awareness of vast surveillance, a growing urge to duck and run. *Move*, target! He pushed forward against people, words, camera flashes.

"*Westhaven Forum*, Mr. Duqayne." The long hair and love beads spelled local campus. "Some of the students threw some pretty rough accusations at you today. One of them even used the words, *liar* and *traitor*."

"Oh God, why won't they leave him alone!" complained Lillian. Mike moved to lead her out of the crowd, but she signaled him to wait.

"I've had more tangible things thrown at me than mere opinions," Duqayne retorted.

"That article you wrote made a lot of waves, Mr. Duqayne. You got people pretty worked up about these super-mutations. My question is this: What made you suddenly change your mind? It it true that the politicians don't want a panic on their hands?"

A distended red sunball squatted on the moss-frescoed roofs. The green-robed halls of learning and the Moorish-pillared arcades under leaning shadows of eucalyptus and pepper trees held a charisma of the old, the established, the traditional; an ivied anchorage of reason.

"Is it true that somebody *got* to you, Mr. Duqayne? Or are you afraid of what you've flushed out and so you're taking an ostrich dive?"

"Somebody *did* get to me, but it wasn't the politicians. It was a long line of scholars. . . ."

Finally there were just the three of them on the walkway and Mike saying something about seeing them tomorrow, and Lillian protesting that tonight would be the informal announcement, and she had counted on him.

"Mike's still a working man," put in Duqayne. "Didn't I tell you? He's going to support us both."

And when they were alone, still moving toward the street, Lillian expressed some personal fears. "You sound like you still haven't made up your mind about Dad's offer. He says you'd be an asset, so—"

"I know how you feel, honey. You'd like to see me land in one spot and stay there."

"David, you *don't* want to be tied down, *do* you! You still have this crazy case on your mind!"

"Lil, believe me, it's too deadly to be crazy."

She saw Brockway overtaking them. "Does Dr. Brockway feel the same way?"

"He doesn't *know* what I know—now skip it!"

"Well, here we are now," boomed Brockway, looming like a teddy bear going to the fair. "Sorry to keep you waiting!" He checked his wristwatch briefly. "My car is just across the street!"

Brockway leading them toward the curb, bantering lightly about retirement—perhaps a private research grant or two—and the solar spotlight shafting its fretful beam through a malevolent skrim of red haze —a filtered other reality seen by an alien eye. . . .

Duqayne stepped off the curb first, and he heard Lillian scream. He remembered the two swarthy faces under twin homburgs in the big black sedan as it bore down upon him with deliberate aim. Instinctively, he reversed his forward motion, but not far enough. A chrome-steel juggernaut gave him a monolithic kick, and his naked spirit rolled into the gutter. His mind, or soul, or some shell-less entity that was himself lay there staring up at faces.

"Oh my God!" somebody exclaimed. "Look at his head!"

Horns. Shouting. College students running toward him. And Lillian staring down, too shocked for tears, struggling to reach out her hand.

Brockway looming. "Don't touch him, Lillian! Don't raise him up, he'll hemorrhage all the more!"

As she finally broke into tears, calling out his name, Brockway looked down at him as cabalistically as a dead moon, fading slowly, slowly, below his darkening horizons. . . .

Poor Lillian! was Duqayne's next to last thought. She had waited so long and patiently for those golden bells. *The bells, bells, bells . . . oh the ringing and the jangling—*

No tears, Irving Brockway? No sorrow at all for

a friend and colleague who is about to die?

 . . . *The tintinnabulation of the bells, bells,*
bells. . . .

CHAPTER 3:
Dark Corners

A dark meteor split the chill thinness of the stratosphere expending a hundred thousand horsepower as it clove its way from the continental divide to Los Angeles in twenty-two minutes. The Hart AFX-500 jet fighter rolled lazily in one giant loop from the Medicine Bow to El Segundo, spurning the ground miles as though they were scattered chaff. Suddenly the delta wings angled out. Dyhedral lifted and arched with the grace of an albatross. The wide flaps dropped, thrust downward by hydraulic arms against the screaming wind.

Among the synthetic extensions of man, thought Mike, was speed—speed of movement and calculation, creating an environment which only a computerized magnification of the thinking process could cope with. The pilot had to surrender now to the ILS system and let the multimillion-dollar experimental bird find its way down the invisible path to its destination. Only the green glow of signal lights on the clustered panel told him that hundreds of machine-instrument events were taking place properly in the nano-second universe of computer, radar, and telemetry. The experience left one with a simultaneous sense of power and futility. Man's towering ingenuity made him a plodding insect among his monuments.

The long multi-storied acres of Hart International rolled by imperiously, giving him a sense of having been summoned, rather than requested, to return tonight from Washington. Yet John Anthony Hart would not have "summoned" him; the man was dynamic but had a saving grace of humility in relation to his personal friends. He was more like a stern father-image to Mike Havelin; had been ever since Mike's teen years when he and Dave had courted

Lillian, back in the simpler days when the Hart family home had been merely a middle-class mansion in the older Highland-Wilshire district. The years seemed long since those days, probably because of the interminable war in Vietnam, yet the single decade in which Hart had pyramided his global industry was a miracle of brevity. From a mere local millionaire, dabbling in aerospace electronics, old J.A. had rocketed his way to becoming a Wall Street phenomenon among the titans—on of the "Blue Chip" top ten.

As the jet lurched to a stop on the apron and the canopy sang open, G2-type faces loomed, glint-eyed and lantern-jawed. Hairy red rocky hands reached in to help him, not that he needed assistance in spite of the pressurized flight suit.

"Real fast passage, Havelin."

"A good thing. Hart wants you upstairs, but *now!*"

Mike popped back his helmet and squinted a smile. "How are the Dodgers doing?"

Deadpans—no take.

"Okay, okay."

A goggled grin and a hand wave dismissed the unknown pilot. He had an impression of urgent movement in custody, down off the plane between shoulder clusters. A man-feel surge, a no-levity aura. It was military, part of his own long experience on ships and in missile battery bunkers—but why here? A fluorescent-gleaming factory escarpment swallowed him into battleship halls. . . .

Desuiting in the flight locker room, on with the green khaki jumper, escorted into the baleful eye-glare of security guards. The phone call, the name check, the card check; the red stripe for Secret Clearance made hands press hidden buttons, causing sliding doors to open, finally giving awesome access—alone and unescorted—to the penthouse elevator.

It was routine to Mike, a past way of life, though strange when related to John Anthony Hart's operation. In the six months since Dave's accident, this whole atmosphere had been stepped up in nervously subtle and disconcertingly effective ways. Even Senator Cain was unexplainedly flittering in and out of the situation. Somehow it all seemed timed with Dave's getting clobbered by that black sedan, but it hadn't solved the immediate problem. Through the impersonal processing and the lonely elevator ride, Mike concentrated on a swift review of the status quo; an instinctive preparation for imminent events. Something, it appeared, was definitely "up"—either a break or a crisis.

Dave Duqayne's tragic accident had thrown him into a coma, and that's where he still was, after six months of every medical-surgical aid that Hart's vast resources could provide. Lillian was withdrawn, wide-eyed in distant reproach; uncommunicative, slowly wasting away. J. A. Hart was fundamentally angered, helpless in the midst of an empire to pull Dave out of his cataleptic state. Yet also, it had seemed to Mike that Hart was glumly reticent about something he knew and feared, or which he was trying to reject as improbable. Meanwhile, Hart had put Mike on the payroll as a security consultant directly out of his office. The assignments had been drummed up largely by Mike, not Hart—seemingly blind alleys that Mike believed in, but which Hart seemed to want to reject, or to "clear from our minds, once and for all, so that we can concentrate on the *facts!*"

Facts?

The matter of Wishnow, for example. Lillian had told him Duqayne's wild story. The real Wishnow was supposed to be a corpse. CIA wouldn't deliver any clues but assured him that Captain Wishnow was alive and well. As for Irving Brockway, Hart especially rejected Mike's suspicions in that area; nevertheless he hadn't blocked Mike's investigations. He had just learned in Washington that the enigmatic microbiologist was on a new classified project at M.I.T. Where had he *really* come from? His PSQ was a taboo item in federal security—strictly no peek, no "need to know."

Who in the hell *was* he? In fact, Mike had a god-awful hunch that Dr. Irving Brockway not only had swallowed the Maltese Falcon, as Lil put it, but he was also, in actual fact, a—

"Mike! Thank God you're here!" Diminutive, wiry J.A. was there when the doors opened, his hand extended, a set expression of "now" on his sharp-planed, coil-spring face.

"Good thing I'm on payroll with a clearance," Mike commented, shaking the vibrant leathery hand and stepping forth. "I'd never have lived through your fancy dip-tank downstairs."

"Sorry for the cloak and dagger. You'll understand someday. Just now I've got some big news and a decision to make."

He followed the brisk figure in the famous shiny-worn brown suit, mentally chuckling at the small tycoon's inextinguishable energy and stubborn fixity of purpose. Followed him through the empty plush reception foyer, past the PBX and potted palms, through gold-tinted glass doors into the Inner Sanctum; a deceptively luxurious split-level abode that seemed dedicated more to creature self-indulgence than to business, with its long deep lounges, oversized low-squat coffee tables, low-key indirect lighting, and small but sumptuous bar. Yet Mike knew the place was ingeniously plugged in to everywhere, through direct wires, data links, time-shared computer banks; even satellites, concentrating in one room an invisible control matrix that was ultra-global in its scope. A camouflaged NORAD.

As for bogeys on the blip-finder, there sat Brockway bigger than life, somberly brooding over his unlighted briar hod. Near him was Lillian, pale, austere, practically in mourning, but not quite as listless as usual. There was a dry-eyed intensity to her; a waiting instinctive brittleness of suspense in her taut expression. A swift signal of relief reached out from her as he entered.

"Well for the love of—!" Mike stopped at the

blue-carpeted stairs leading downward into the low, broad room. "Brockway! They told me in Washington—"

"Hart's hand on his arm urged him down the shallow steps. "What they told you, and what I can get out of my old buddy, Senator Cain, are two different ballgames. We dug up Brock and it wasn't hard. He was on his way here, anyway. He has some news, Mike. I think it's a break for Dave—I want you to listen to him."

It didn't all start that quickly. The world's most highspeed people are still subject to human amenities, such as a J&B on the rocks, which proved Mike to be no exception. Or was it, he thought, a subliminal tradition of the jousting pits? A base ground for battle girding? Brockway kept watching him; Lil eyed them both apprehensively; and Hart rapidly laced the gap with lead-ins. Mainly about Dave: how he'd flown in top brain specialists and neurosurgeons from all over the world, let them use the corporation's most advanced medical facilities. But not one of them could do a thing.

"Hell!" the little man snorted in his frustration. "We even brought in the *Bug,* direct from the Ranch —" He stopped, suddenly staring rather egg-facedly at Brockway.

Brock smirked laconically. "An 'oops' for *you,* J.A."

"Sorry. That was a slip."

"Why?" Mike knifed in deliberately.

Hart's pale blue eyes scanned him wistfully as though there were much more he wished he might reveal. "Forgive me, Mike. That's still top drawer."

"So if I'm going to really swing into this case," retorted Mike, "I'll need a Black Button. Right?"

Hart and Brockway answered him with a mutual silence. It was the practiced deadpan of the Black Button boys—the highest security classification in the book.

"All right," he conceded with a weary tone of resentment, "so I get to rain-dance all around the edges. But I warn you, I'll make damn good use of what I've got!"

Hart smiled in grim appreciation. "To an enemy, that *would* be a threat. We know what you've got, Mike, or you wouldn't be here." Catching Brock's quizzical stare, Hart explained. "Mike's native powers of deduction are not quick, Irving, but they are ponderous. Sooner or later I think he's going to lay out the Gordian knot on an analog board, strand by strand. Dave swears he's a genius in that respect. A poor man's Sherlock Holmes with the instincts of a hound of the Baskervilles. He strikes at the throat!"

Brockway studied his briar, giving it a fresh fill from his battered pouch. "Then it's too bad he's been wasting his talents on a vintaged if not odoriferous red herring. . . ."

"What? You mean my question about what happened to Dave. . . ?"

Brock's fathomless black eyes pivoted toward Mike with the impact of a granite Colossus. He had a flash impression of put-down by a towering presence. The voice was deep, abysmal. "I'd like to dissolve this dangerous *myth* concerning paranormal or alien influences in the case of one David Duqayne. As I and Senator Cain have emphasized before, the Kettleridge case is closed."

"Of course I'll second the motion on *that*," put in Hart, glancing with a certain degree of hopefulness at Mike.

"Not in *my* book!" Mike slung out stubbornly, mindful of David and Goliath. "It's the same as murder. Whoever paid off those goons in the black sedan—"

"Stop it!" cried Lillian suddenly. They all stared at her. When Hart approached her with a gesture of fatherly supplication, she waved him off. "Oh, Dad, please!"

"What's the matter, Lillian? We're *doing* everything we can!"

"I mean—our self-deception . . . you, me, Mike—

all of us!" She struggled for cry-control. "We have to face facts as they are. David has been in a coma for half a year. They've given him up. There's nothing *anybody* can do. . . . He's beyond our help; science, money—even love!"

Her eyes pleaded for Mike's understanding and his heart went through the grinder—very rare Salisbury.

"I can't even give him that!" she resumed. "I've tried to reach through to him. I swear he knows I'm there. It's torture for him. He's slowly dying, unable to speak!"

"Please, Lil." Mike pleaded for a lifeline. "Take it easy, baby!"

"Now look, Lillian!" J.A. protested. "This is certainly no time to give up hope! You've heard about the connection Brock has made with Dr. Borg. It's even in today's paper—look!"

"Oh I know," she retorted impatiently. "He showed it to me when he came in."

"Let me see that." Mike took the front-page sheet of the L.A. *Times* out of Hart's hands. But he did a take, watching Lil as she looked strangely into corners and appeared to shudder instinctively. She wore a familiar beaded necklace that terminated in a large chunk of turquoise; a weirdly symbolical fetish she had sometimes referred to as her "Freya" beads. She was clutching the turquoise as though it were a bane of evil.

Brock looked at his watch. "It's late," he said. "I've briefed you on Borg—all I can. You transmit it to Mike, and make up your minds."

"Just a minute, fellas!"

Hart and Brockway turned to stare at Mike, who met their quizzical gaze with a G.I. glare and a stubborn jaw that raised angry muscle bumps.

"J.A., you threw me a cozy bouquet concerning my powers of deduction. I don't know about that, but I'll tell you this much: Something smells!"

"Now Mike," Hart started to protest.

"Sit down, dammit! Both of you!"

Lil's eyes went wide as she stared at him wonderingly. Hart and Brock exchanged glances. The biggest thing they could do was break into a patronizing grin of mutual amusement. "Mike," said Hart, almost unctuously, "you're stretching it, boy. We'll talk, after Brockway leaves."

"That's all right, John," put in Brockway, looming rather testily over the scene. "If Havelin has something to say, we may as well clear the air, once and for all. He has that 'Hound of the Baskervilles' look."

The two men made an elaborate project of sitting down. "All right, Mike," said Hart, waving a hand. "You asked for equal time on TV. This is it. Spill it!"

"Thank you, J.A.—but Dr. Irving Brockway won't like it." Mike paced the floor, watching Brock warily as he moved in on him, full bore. "It should be obvious that we haven't *begun* to talk. I'm sorry to say it, but in my mind Irv Brockway has a lot of explaining to do. And frankly, I don't dig this hurried-up brush-off!"

Hart began to glower at him. "Get to the point, Mike."

"All right. The point is this: Don't push the closure of the Kettleridge case down my throat because I'm *not* going to swallow it—I don't go for a shove, and that's what I'm getting. I told you I'd use what I've got!"

"Mister Havelin." Brockway used his special-power tone now the impressive brows lowering effectively. "You could improve your prosecuting technique considerably if you would learn to paraphrase. Mr. Hart has asked you to get to the point. It is obvious to me that you have an axe to grind in regard to myself. Why don't you get it off your chest?"

"Fine! In a nutshell, Doctor, the K-chromosome research is the great common denominator here. You are in the middle, sir, and Dave Duqayne was the patsy. In Dave's book, Wishnow is a corpse!"

Hart shook his head, obviously trying to launch Mike a warning signal. "That's ridiculous!"

"Come on, J.A. *I'm* on the air, remember? Dave *deliberately* scratched Wishnow's face to get a skin and blood sample. I reported this to you, John, in full detail. When Dr. Chafey made an analysis he got the Kettleridge treatment, only this time with a bomb. Then Dave got clobbered by two goons in a black sedan. He knew he was a target, and they got him!"

"I'm still waiting, Havelin," boomed Brockway. "Where do I come in?"

"Let's put it this way. You don't go *out* until you do some explaining. You strained a hernia to kibosh Dave's theory—only a couple thousand blood samples, with you in control of the project! What the hell is that? What about your own blood, Brockway? Did you sample yourself? Or would you lay odds that Hart's medical boys wouldn't come up with any Rh-U antibodies where you are concerned?"

"Mike," said Hart, with an ominous calmness. "I have Senator Cain's personal clearance for Dr. Brockway. Now I think that the recommendation of the U.S. Senate Committee on National Security—"

"Nevertheless," Brockway interrupted, "this seems to be enough of a question in your minds to deserve a final proof. I'll be glad to submit a blood sample."

"Don't be ridiculous!" Hart exclaimed, getting to his feet. "Now come along! I know you have more important things to attend to!"

Brock shrugged, also getting up.

"Brockway?" Mike pursued stubbornly. "Why can't I get a clear statement from Washington in regard to your present project with M.I.T.?"

Brock raised an innocent brow. "It's not top drawer, actually. Simply a matter of the national ecology—industrial pollution problems. You've heard about the panic over mercury poisoning. I'm simply dabbling in old-fashioned embryonics . . . chromosome statistics." He looked at his watch again.

52

Hart took his arm. "Come on, Brock. I know you've got to get back."

"*Doctor* Brockway. . . ."

Brock paused. He and Mike and Hart all stared at Lillian. "Tell me, when were you born?"

Brock searched her face, then Hart's, somewhat off balance. Hart waved a hand impatiently at her. "Now Lillian, this is no time for your astrology!"

"She's an astrologer?" Brock swung his gaze to her with a curiously changed brand of intentness.

"All I'm asking is, when were you born?" she insisted.

As Hart again started to protest, Brock lifted his pipe to silence him. He seemed unusually meditative, then he grinned. "It would be a giveaway, you know. We older bachelors tend to hide those things."

"Doctor, when were you born?"

The vast dark eyes deepened in their shadows under the hirsute brows. "Long before sunrise, child. The sheep were asleep in the meadow." He seemed to savor the symbology as though patronizing her.

"Yes. Well, so much for that!" put in Hart impatiently. "Come on, Brock, I'll see you to the elevator." As the two started toward the low-fanned staircase, Hart paused. He sniffed the air curiously. "Do you smell sulphur in here?"

Dead silence. All sniffed. Brock puffed his pipe. No sulphur as far as Lil and Mike were concerned.

"Damn!" ejaculated Hart. "If any more of that vulcanizing operation gets into the air-conditioning, I'll make them sub-contract the S-15! Come on, Brock!"

The two men exited through the golden doors and Mike and Lillian were overwhelmingly alone in the wide, plush, low-ceilinged room. Their eyes met urgently.

"Mike!" she whispered, coming swiftly into his arms. "Oh my God, help me or I'll flip my ever-loving gourd!"

He kissed her mindlessly. "Forgive me, honey.

Blame it on astrology, but your *need*—just bleeds me dry."

She tried gentle resistance in spite of desperation for the comfort of an intimate friend. "You're not a water sign," she told him, in close-aura face-flush and a perfumed cataract of brunette hair that cowled them both in a hush of wonder. The devil's elixir was between them, so agonizingly borrowed. "Oh Mike, I'm scared!"

He died a number of times just holding the soft female essence of her; close to her blue eyes, her shining lips. Mentally he said a graffito but it didn't help. He had to play the hypocrite; the staunch, square-jawed buddy-hero in a triangle that marked him for Hell. "You know what I feel like?" he said. "I'd like to kick in a door, or maybe throw something."

"I know. I've felt it, too."

"What kind of a crack is that?"

"There's an evil here. I've sensed it."

"You were clutching your witch beads and staring into the corners. What was that all about?"

"Mike, maybe I'm crazy, but I've felt strange all evening. As though somebody were watching me take a bath through a knothole. Even . . . even. . . ." She pressed a burning cheek against his chest. "I can't say it!"

His hands on her arms tightened in gentle insistence. "Even what, Lil?"

She glanced down at her necklace and again clutched the turquoise pendant. She broke away from him, pacing slowly, staring at the carpet as though at a ritualistic pentacle of Solomon. "Mike, I've *seen* the essence of evil before—this is how I know."

"What do you mean, you've seen evil?"

She turned to him, solemn-eyed. "Witchcraft, the covens, the conjurations."

"Aw come *on* now, baby! I mean, playing Ouija board and crystal ball is nice for parlor games, but—"

"Dave asked me once, point-blank, if I was a witch."
She seemed not to hear, staring through or beyond
him. "I told him no—that there was a certain commitment I couldn't make. But the real reason was
Cyprian and Melusina."

"Who?"

She focused her eyes on him suddenly, shook her
head, and sat down. "I'm sorry. I'm not being co-
herent. Those are symbolic names for the leaders of
the coven I was starting to get into. I don't want to
break oaths, but—you remember Larry, the young
man you used to contact for underground information, the one I introduced to you and David on that
narcotics case?"

"What about Larry?"

"He's a full warlock, a high priest."

"*That* hippie acid-head?"

"He's off the drug trips. They spoil his natural
psychic gift. He's very powerful, especially when
working with Melusina. That's Heidi, the high priestess. Once we asked the two of them to materialize an
elemental—"

"A what?"

"An elemental. A group materialization of very
dangerous atavistic forces in the sub-levels of consciousness."

"You're losing me, Lil."

"There are very terrible ancient things; mysteries
of evolution of the human psyche, a million years
before Babylon and Chaldea. We came up a level or
two in all that time, but the Id of the primordial is
still there."

"Lil, you've got to be putting me on!"

"Just take my word for it, Mike. I *saw* that thing,
whatever it was, and a roomful of dedicated mystics
screaming to have it removed from their sight. I'll
not describe it, but what I felt then I felt tonight
while Brockway was here."

"Oh, you did? Tell me more."

She got up again, pacing back and forth and

occasionally nibbling her cuticles. "It was as if . . . some unseen intelligence was searching my secret thoughts . . . silently picking my brains . . . and with such a sweaty aura of absolute evil that somehow I feel stained inside. Mike! Ever since Dave was struck down, I think I've been losing my mind!"

"You know, Lil, sometimes you come on like technicolor—all different shades. When Dave told you the weird stuff he had on his mind, you put him down like you didn't buy a single word. But, knowing what you say you do, and having witnessed a few manifestations along the same lines, which side are you on?"

"Mike, I just don't want to believe the handwriting on the wall. I'm afraid for myself. I mean, accepting a reality like that—I could change, Mike. I could *change!* I shudder to think—"

"Then *don't* think. You're all up-tight. Dave's situation has given you a case of the creeping wheemies. All that bell, book and candle stuff has given your imagination the wrong kind of pabulum. Why don't you just relax and climb down off of that broomstick!"

"I wish I could do exactly that."

He strove to change the subject. "Incidentally, what was that astrology bit all about? Brockway's birth date. I thought he acted funny."

"It wasn't funny. That was the most frightening element of all, if I've got nerve enough to accept the message."

"What message?"

"Born before the sunrise. Astrologically, he referred to the Ascendant—Aries—the Vernal Equinox. I think he did, anyway."

"So?"

"And the 'sheep' asleep in the meadow. Aries the Ram, and his harem."

"You're way out there, kid. I'm no astrologer. What's the translation?"

She collected herself with a visible effort. "Maybe

you're right, Mike. I'm all up-tight and, well, I just hope my imagination has been playing tricks. But sometime when you think you can trust my sanity, ask me about the Vernal Equinox."

"All right, Lil. I'll do that." He lit up his pipe, forcing himself to sit down and pick up the L.A. *Times*. There was a slight tremor in his hands. Subconscious empathy? Premonition? He squared his shoulders stubbornly and kept his gaze from the dark corners. To hell with it, he thought. No use both of them spilling their marbles. "So what's with this Dr. Borg? His name was brought up before, you know. Your dad said Senator Cain had suggested him."

A typical European egghead stared insolently back at him from the front page, replete with beard and tonsure. *June 15,* NIGHT FINAL: ECCENTRIC GENIUS MAKES RARE APPEARANCE ... *Los Angeles. —Reputed as being the world's foremost brain specialist and neurosurgeon, Dr. Jules Borg made an unscheduled appearance today during a special seminar in advanced surgical techniques, held at the University of California at Westwood.*

Lillian sat down silently beside him and helped him scan the article.

"Hmm. Where's he been hiding?" grunted Mike. "'Mysterious recluse ... special surgical techniques normally withheld as *proprietary*' ... *!*"

"Mike, he scares me."

He searched her pale countenance and offered no comfort. He couldn't.

She got up nervously and went to the bar. "I need a drink!"

"I'll join you," he said, and followed her.

When Hart came back into the room he found them huddled glumly at the bar. "Come on, kids!" he insisted. "We've found our man, haven't we? If Dr. Borg can't help Dave—"

"How much is the ante?" Mike asked.

"What, Borg? Seventy-five thousand. But considering what it might mean to us—"

"Seventy-five *thou!* My God! That's enough to put *me* in a coma!"

"Mike, we mentioned Borg before. After Senator Cain suggested that Brockway might be able to persuade him, you did a little leg-work on him. What did you come up with?"

"He operates rarely, but when he does it's some kind of surgical landmark. A hard one to stir out of seclusion. How come Brockway could swing him?"

"Academic connections, mainly, but with some State Department assistance."

"Now there's another thing, J.A. You and Cain and Brockway have bent yourselves out of shape to close the book on the Kettleridge case. So why the government's interest in Dave?"

Hart's face clouded momentarily. "A personal favor, that's all. The Senator and I were classmates." His pale blue eyes met Mike's and Lil's gaze challengingly, perhaps stubbornly. Lil knew her father's expressions. That tight little pull-down on the left side of his compressed lips always accentuated his chin cleft. It meant he had made up his mind.

Mike puffed laboriously on his pipe.

"Mike, when you start sending up smoke signals with that coal-burner of yours, there's something brewing. Are you still chasing bogeymen?"

"No." Mike threw a cryptic signal to Lillian. "Just poking around in a few dark corners . . . thinking about Dave. . . ."

At mention of Dave, Lil turned away, but not soon enough to conceal the tiny glimmer of a tear. . . .

∞

He had only imagined the smouldering desolation that one stood in, unable to scream; it was a metaphor. But now this was really it! He knew he was alive and he knew that the doctors and nurses knew he was alive, if you could call it that. A more proper name was catalepsy. Edgar Allen Poe had termed it premature burial. He wasn't under the ground yet, but maybe this was worse. Day after day, week after week, alive and staring, even hearing everything that was said around him but not being able to move a muscle or to feel. A silently screaming bubble of tortured consciousness, locked in Limbo.

Evidently, Lillian and her father were going all out. This was a John Anthony Hart foundation, an advanced neurosurgical research institute employing specialists and equipment that no reasonable insurance policy could touch. Once he had been hooked up to a 1984 brain-probe machine, which was referred to in hushed tones as the "Bug." From under his skull, about two dozen wires had sent "analog-to-digital" converted messages into a computer in the basement. Doctors and myopic egghead assistants had prodded him, administered drugs, applied reflex shocks to "locomotor centers" of his body; and sometimes he had become aware of that transistorized Cellar Creature sending back "digital-to-analog" commands. The precise, insistent data input had produced a shrieking *will* to move, to writhe, to kick and dance or shout; but nothing had happened. Somewhere there was an abyss between the entity of David Duqayne and his body.

During other programmed tests, Lillian or Mike or J.A. himself, or all three together, were there looking down at him—Lillian's eyes a desolation of rubbled hope; Mike's square-jawed face a faithful beacon at the bridge-end of life, seen dimly across a widening gulf; and J. Anthony Hart, a stubborn promontory against the tempest, his lean, craggy countenance a study of frustrated power, a Merlin of millions unable to cast his accustomed spell upon the tide. At first, when the bandages were off his eyes and he could sometimes see Lillian, she had shown occasional signs of courage and confidence. Then he would catch a glimpse of her weeks later, and she would be without makeup and dressed somberly as though for a funeral. The last time he saw her he knew that she and Mike were holding hands. Was it mutual sympathy over loss of a comrade? Or a growing new instinct that cast a shadow of the inevitable? At first he had strained to see either one of them or hear their voices, but now he wished they would go away and forget him and he cursed the hideous paradox of human charity that could torture with good intent, doggedly preserving a life that prayed to be spent.

There were other times—at night and with the bandages pressing tightly against his eyelids—when his thoughts were projected against an infinite dark screen. At these times he dreaded the cyclic upsurge of hope, that cruel deception that leaped beyond reality, gorging on the mirage of survival. What was it Poe had said about catalepsy? "A certain period elapses, and some unseen principle again sets in motion the magic pinions and the wizard wheels. The silver cord was not forever loosed, nor the golden bowl irreparably broken. But where, meantime, was the soul?"

Then there were the cogent periods of insistent memory when he was forced to review his entire connection and experience with the Kettleridge case. The conclusion was always inescapable. Mathematics had convinced modern astronomers that the universe must harbor at least two hundred million worlds comparable to Earth, or even more advanced. Statistically, then, it was a more remote possibility to *escape* exterior contact than not; especially over a span of tens of thousands of years. There *were* K-chromosome types abroad in the world; they were mutant descendants of the star-gods or some warped resultant of matings with earthwomen—maybe a combination of both, as quote Genesis 6:4. They had been around for uncounted ages, and maybe old Charles Fort was right: "We are property," he had said. This was his legacy after a lifetime of probing into the unexplained *(Lo! —Strange Worlds—The Book of the Damned)*. Fort was right, so was Kettleridge, and now so was *he;*

but where it had gotten any of those who *knew?* "Property"—a marvelous word for futility.

He damned his logic and questioned his morality when he thought of his decision to use the marriage to Lillian as a camouflage. Of course he loved her, and because of it he had deftly dodged the idea of matrimony—up to the moment of shock over the museum episode and Dr. Chafey's death. Why not, he had thought at the time, use the college confab as a platform for a public denial of his previous convictions, and cover his trail with a honeymoon? During a few brief years of bliss not otherwise obtainable, he could build his traps; and then one day— But maybe *they* were mind readers. They got to him. Those two in the black sedan who ran him down had the look of Mafia. But what connection could the underworld have with these Overlords, whoever they were?

And where did Brockway *really* fit into the picture? When the results of Kettleridge's autopsy hit the fan, the first security man to appear on the scene had Brockway in tow; and it was a short step from there to the secret project on K-chromosome research. He never did get all of his background—something about M.I.T. and past distinctions in biochemistry, on scientific advisory boards, and in chemical warfare research. That's about as far as information could be stretched when you were dealing with inside government types. For all he knew, Dr. Irving Brockway could be CIA or a foreign agent. He liked Lillian's simile the best, about the Maltese Falcon. He could have let it go at that if it were not for his instincts about people. Where Brockway was concerned, he sensed an undercurrent of vast personal power, something camouflaged and deliberately held in reserve. He was probably not a K-chromosome type, however, because he never caused Duqayne's ears to start ringing. Then why, sometimes, did Brockway's deep surveillance raise the hackles on him? Instinct raised the warning signal, but as yet there was no answer. And maybe now there never would be. . . .

Mike was bugged by the surprising appearance of Brockway the next day at the medical briefing prior to Dave's final operation. Hart had arranged the confab since the J.A. Hart Medical Foundation was his to command, as was the special medical staff. Mike and Lillian were permitted to sit there in the paneled conference room and listen, through a very soporific summer afternoon, though most of the medical discussion was over their heads—ventriculography, pneumoencephalography, cerebral angiography, the perils of the transparent pia arachnoid, trephines, rongeurs, ad infinitum. The great Dr. Borg had made his examinations and recommendations. He was due to appear and supervise preparing the patient at 4:00 P.M. It was now 3:30 P.M. and the meeting was breaking up. The advanced staff had been deeply impressed by Borg. He was officially sanctioned.

Again surprisingly, Brock was much more friendly than he had been in Hart's office. He even went out of his way to reassure Lillian. "I know Borg sounds mysterious," he boomed at her in his most mellow tone. "But believe me, he's far ahead of his time. If there is any man alive—"

"Thank you," she told him, and she was puzzled.

Hart grinned at the hard, busy puffs Mike made with his pipe, but it appeared that the matter was settled and he had to rush off to another meeting. The foundation's director, Dr. Lanis, discussed Brock's government project for a moment or two, since his own specialty lay in the same area of research; something about "enzyme electrostatics and molecular techniques."

Lil tugged at Mike's sleeve. "I want to see David," she urged, "before that *doctor* arrives."

There were handshakes, good-byes, and Brock and J.A. were off to other worlds, leaving Mike and Lillian alone in a gleaming, antiseptic corridor. Dr. Lanis had given permission. They could see Dave until Borg arrived to prepare him for brain surgery.

"If you don't mind being expelled by a genius," Lanis had smiled, "you'll find he's not bashful."

"Anybody who charges seventy-five grand can't be bashful," grumbled Mike. Then he concentrated on Lillian. He knew she needed moral support. "Well, Lil, no dark corners today?"

"That's just it!" she answered. "Before, in Dad's office, Brockway was positively creepy!"

"To me, he always will be!"

They arrived at Dave's room and went in. . . .

She caught her breath at the sight of David without hair. They had shaved him cleanly for the trephining. He lay there motionlessly with a bandage across his eyes. Mike rejected the vision of a firing squad, a distant roll of drums. Lil just stood there looking down at Dave in oblivion.

He couldn't stand seeing Dave in his helplessness, and Lillian in her all-too-private grief. He glared through the slats of the venetian blinds at the wide-sweeping rainbirds out on the lawn. They were Fate-nymph materializations in some surrealistic fantasia, swirling glittering diamond veils in the late-afternoon sun. He clamped down hard on an empty pipe and drove his thoughts away from Dave and Lil—which left him the long-shadowed Kettleridge affair, and Irving Brockway. Pieces that didn't fit together became itch-worms in his marrow. Something tugged at the back of his mind—a wisp of memory, disconnected conversations. He knew the instinct and never belittled it. If he kept at it there would be a sudden synthesis. But something warned him he wouldn't like it.

Mike became aware of her standing beside him, also staring out at the ghostly rainbirds. Christ! If she'd only just bawl or sob or cry—but *staring* that way! "Lil!" he said urgently.

She looked at him listlessly, her eyes and lips almost feverishly dry.

"Now look, honey, you're beating yourself over the head. Today is the big day. . . ."

∞

In his world of waiting darkness, Duqayne could hear them. He couldn't move a muscle to let them know it. Not one synapse would discharge a message to his articulatory system. No slightest murmur or twitch of the lips was possible. But oh how excruciatingly bright the mind!—how clear and sensitive the aural channels that brought him their voices in a symphony of nuance! Lillian in her up-tight submission to grief; Mike in his posture of faithful friend. It *was* grief; it *was* friendship—but his tortured reasoning ripped the scales between good and bad. He loved them; he hated them. It wasn't jealousy, for Christ's sake, it was pain. *God,* make them go away and leave him to death's transition! He screamed and flailed, silently and motionlessly, in a fever of cowardice, emotionally incapable of witnessing their encounter here in his presence. Yet he could not escape.

"Your wedding day has a nasty interruption. But now we'll get Dave back on his feet for good." A pause; no sound from Lillian. "And I *mean*—back to Earth. All that other malarkey will be forgotten. You'll see."

Good old Mike. Still in there covering for him, damn his leatherneck hide! Take her away!

"He was almost back to Earth, wasn't he?"

Her voice brought visions of two-toned loveliness, breasts crescent-cupped by a bedlamp, soft lips, the melony softness against him and her urgent possessiveness. "I could have brought him in for a landing if there had been a honeymoon. But now there never will be."

So that's what she thought of Borg. He clutched

fondly at the death-wish corroboration, hoping it would all end soon.

"Lil, I'm going to give you an order. This is no good. Now you shape up or I'll have to do it for you."

"The hell you say! *You* don't know what I'm going through!" A sound of choked words, very near—*too* near to his bedside. "You and your great deductive calm and your eternal pipe! You have no right, Mike Havelin, to tell me what to do. I'm only human!"

"And so am I! How much more of this do you think *I* can take?"

That's what I'm yelling at you, Mike! In the name of all that's holy—take her out of here!

Mike's voice was practically on top of him. "What kind of torture do you think it is . . . watching you, week after week, knocking yourself to pieces—and me standing by helpless to help you—to reach *you* with love!"

Duqayne strained to control his conscious mind, to go blank and not hear. But it went on.

"Oh, I don't mean intrusion, Lil. I mean—well, if a poor substitute would help. . . ."

He could practically see their faces; both probably staring at each other in some sort of mutual consternation.

"For God's sake, you know what I mean—what it's always *had* to mean, ever since you and Dave. . . ."

Silence now. He knew what it cost Mike to get this far with his feelings. Taking a machine-gun nest or a pill box would have been easier.

"Look! I'm sorry. It's a sick joke, okay? We're both tangled up, so skip it!"

A stifled sob . . . a rustle of sudden movement.

"Oh Mike! Forgive me!"

Well—and why not? They had both loved her all along. It's over, Mike. Just lead her gently away. Don't worry about your old buddy here. Daddy Hart bought me a high-priced knife—the best present possible. Just a little painless exploration down in the old gray matter, Mike—no pain, you understand. And suddenly the darkness will be void, and peace.

So take her, with blessings, and *sayonara!*

∞

Mike held her gently to him but it was different now than it had been in Hart's office. Dave lying there cooled it. He had no choice but the big brother bit. They looked at each other and he knew that they both knew. She smiled ruefully, with a heart-fibrillating chin-quiver and a fleck of tears.

"Mike, I—" "Lil—"

The simultaneous blurt made them chuckle inadvertently.

"Okay, now look, baby. We haven't given up on Dave *yet*—"

"But you seem to take such a dim view of Dr. Borg."

"He was approved by Hart's whole medical staff, wasn't he?"

"Yes, but you—"

"Oh I know I've been griping. It's just that I don't go for the cloak and dagger bit. If he's such a recluse he must be independent as hell. So what's the seventy-five grand all about? Is he running a racket or something?"

"I don't blame you a bit, young man!"

They were surprised by Borg, himself, who bustled past them to Dave with a small black satchel that might have been standard equipment for a rural G.P. Almost as large as Brockway, he was nevertheless ascetic; scholarly in the European sense, with a very pale round face, bald head, an incongruously priestly black tonsure, and a meticulous Van Dyke. The eyes were small, coal black, and alive with a glint of challenge behind their inscrutability. "The fee is outrageous," he continued, "but so is the patient's condition. Have we met?"

Mike made introductions and the black eyes lingered penetratingly on Lillian for a moment when he learned who she was. But he covered suddenly. "Ah yes! Mike

Havelin. You're a private investigator. That medical racket in San Diego. I—ah—have received considerable information about you—also about your associate here."

"That doesn't make us even," Mike retorted testily.

"However, you've investigated, of course."

"Well—you *are* a member of the AMA."

"Ah! Then all this is legal!" Borg removed the bandage from David's eyes. The eyes stared ceilingward, unmoving. He carefully wiped cold perspiration from Dave's forehead. "Mr. Havelin, I will confess. I prefer research, and in order to force a limitation on actual practice I charge a prohibitive fee. A sort of surgical key-club, you might say. In this case, Senator Cain, Mr. Hart, and Dr. Brockway would not be intimidated, so here I am!"

Lillian had been studying Dave's unblinking eyes. "Doctor, they say you've gone into David's case quite thoroughly—"

"Of course, my dear! I won't confuse your pretty head with medical terms, except to say that we have a problem here which affects a little-known sub-complex of the axosomatic neural system—more electrochemical than it is purely physiological. I can tell you this much: I am quite certain the operation will result in a marked improvement."

"I see," she said, in a way that meant she didn't see at all.

"Now if you'll both excuse me I must make some preparations here. They are quite proprietary and I'll have to insist on my prerogatives in that regard." Borg opened his medical case and hesitated meaningfully, waiting for them to leave. However, as Mike made a gesture of leading Lillian out, he added: "Mr. Havelin, do I sound like some sort of a quack?"

Lillian searched Mike's face as though the worthy doctor had aptly expressed her hidden fears.

"Yes, you do, doctor. Your bedside manner is a bit facetious considering a man's life is in your hands— and even my Medical Corps training says you're putting us on with that 'axosomatic' jargon. But—"

The black eyes smouldered briefly. "Perhaps you'd prefer the *real* jargon. Shall we go into the quantum mechanics of molecular reconstructions? Multi-plexed laser techniques, electrostatic regeneration of myto-chondria and myelin, or the magnetodynamics of cel-lular metabolic alterations through the ionic reversal of sodium and potassium potentials? If these processes are unknown to the advanced staff of this institution, I am sure that Miss Hart—"

"Okay, I get the point, Doctor. What I wanted to say was that you *sounded* like a quack. That's what you asked me. I'll have to concede that a graduate from four major medical universities must know what he's doing."

"Thank you." He still waited for them to leave, so they did.

Outside in the corridor, Mike tried to pick up Lil's sagging morale. "We'll know the result tomorrow, honey. In the meantime, I'm taking you out to din-ner. Okay?"

As they walked away, the door latch clicked un-noticed. David's room was effectively locked against intrusion. . . .

∞

He could see the great man. He knew by his bearded smirk that he was aware of his conscious state and would understand what was said to him.

"You knew too much, Duqayne. . . ." The clipped, cultured tones were low, confident, clinical. The pasty scholar's face loomed over him, the dark eyes gleam-ing secretly. "But now that *They* have dismissed you and you are legally a terminal case, I am claiming you for a private experiment of my own. I'm going to bring you back, but first you'll be *wired*. Do you know what that means? The human species is supposed to utilize about ten percent of its gray matter; person-ally I think they're using less than that. In your case, however, you're going to be using *all* of it! That's right. A surgical mutant, a super intelligence possessing the psychic capabilities of our Overlords—extrasensory perception, telekinesis—perhaps even the power of an infant god." Borg deftly prepared a long hypodermic needle and leaned closer. "But under *my* control, Duqayne. Even in cosmic politics there must be a balance of power—and you shall be our bargaining point."

He loomed still closer, the gleaming needle point poised only inches away. "Come now, why sweat it, my friend?" With a ball of gauze, Borg again wiped the sweating forehead. "You are to become a counterweapon, strictly on my own terms."

The needle penetrated the inner corner of Duqayne's left eye. There was a sword-blow of skull-gutting pain, followed by a distant ringing . . . ringing . . . ringing. . . .

∞

Hart's phone rang insistently.

Rather, it might be said that one of six private "J.A." extensions was ringing, and it took a miniskirted PBX girl, and two male secretaries, three full minutes to get through the kind of message that could make him drop his A.M. reports and continuous conferences long enough to answer.

"Now look, Mike," he barked into the phone in his private office behind the penthouse, "they tell me you've got that hospital in an uproar." Male Secretary No. 1 and four V.I.P. visitors saw him frown deeply as he listened; his mood more troubled than his voice seemed to reveal. "Mike! The operation was successful. That's all we should be concerned with for now. . . . No, I haven't been able to contact Borg, and neither has Brockway. But if Borg doesn't want anyone to see the patient—" J.A. swung his head from side to side, apparently struggling to contain his impatience. "Mike—dammit, boy! Will you *stop* waving that cloak and dagger? There's *nothing* fishy, as you put it, about a Do-Not-Disturb sign on the room of

69

a man just out of brain surgery!" He listened, tight-mouthed, eyes slowly widening. The famous finger tap began on the desk. To the initiated, this meant an impending squelch or a sudden turn of decision. Finally, the diminutive tycoon sighed wearily, knowing what this would cost in terms of his daily calendar. "All right, Mike." The tone was resigned. "Tell Lillian I'll come out there and see what I can do. . . ."

"Anything wrong, J.A.?" queried No. 1 as the receiver slowly lowered into its cradle.

The quick brown eyes snapped toward No. 1 and at the assembled V.I.P.s. He seemed to emerge surreptitiously from a trance of secret fear. "I don't think so, Stan, but I'll have to go to the Foundation."

The V.I.P.s rose to their feet in concerted consternation. "But—!"

J.A. checked his watch. "One hour, Stan. You rig the calendar. I'll skip that lunch wrangle with Forsythe Corporation." Having reached for his hat, he turned back. "And Stan, you might establish a channel for Call Three."

"Call *Three*, sir?" No. 1 appeared to pale with the shock of emergency. "Again?"

"Just in case I need it."

And with that, he left the office.

∞

The double glass doors of the main entrance were automatic, but it seemed as though Hart's sheer force of personality had swung them open. He moved in fast, virtually sweeping Dr. Lanis with him. *"You're* right to unlock that door, Lanis!"

"I know, J.A., but we don't make a practice of overriding a doctor's opinion regarding his patient. Dr. Borg's instructions—"

"He's made himself unavailable, and that's unethical under the circumstances. I hired him, dammit, he should stay on tap until I sign him off!"

The insweeping wave of the Hart presence picked up a worried young nurse at the mid-corridor station, and soon they were together with Mike and Lillian at the locked door of Duqayne's room. In contrast to yesterday, Lillian was dressed in a more cheerful outfit, but now her momentary hopefulness had reverted to her instinctive mood of apprehension.

"Hello, kids," Hart greeted them briskly. "I hope we know what the hell we're doing!"

"Now just a moment, please!" insisted Lanis. "You people understand the circumstances. Brain surgery isn't a simple tonsilectomy. You're taking a grave responsibility in violating Dr. Borg's instructions. Miss Carlson, will you kindly repeat those instructions to Mr. Hart?"

The pretty little blonde was obviously on the side of Mike and Lillian. Apparently irked by Borg's overbearing manner, she replied with a touch of professional pique. "Certainly. When he came out of surgery last night, Dr. Borg personally rolled the patient to his room. Then he issued flat instructions that nobody was to see or treat the patient, other than himself. He requested the room key. Then he locked Mr. Duqayne in, and he left." Her eyes appealed widely to Dr. Lanis. "It *is* unorthodox. I mean—no charts, no i.v., no EKG. . . ."

"That will be enough, Miss Carlson," interrupted Lanis.

"No contact with Borg," said Mike glumly. "We've tried for hours."

"I'm sorry to be a baby, Dad," explained Lillian, "but this is too much! The operation was supposed to be successful, and here we can't even *look* at David. How do we know what he might do when he comes out of sedation? Surely he's going to need something—"

"Like a bedpan," suggested the nurse defiantly.

Lanis had the expression of a man suddenly surprised on a wrong-way street. He made one valiant effort to extricate himself. "Miss Hart, your emotions are understandable, but science should be the monitor in this case."

"There are many sciences, Doctor," Mike cut in decisively, "and I've got one of my own. It's called horse sense. Dave Duqayne is a patient, not a prisoner. I say we'd better have a look at him—right now!"

"You have a way of making your point," Hart smiled grimly. Then he frowned suddenly, the brown eyes stabbing a warning. "But if you're wrong, Mike —"

"I grew up with Dave. He'd want me to take the chance."

Hart's analytical glare swiveled to Lanis. "All right. I own this foundation, so ethically you're covered. You have the master key. Open it!"

Lanis shrugged. He extracted a small key case and finally unlocked the disputed door. Mike and Lillian were the first to enter.

The room was empty. The bed had not been occupied. Lillian stared at it, frozen. Mike checked the open window and then came back to face Lanis, Hart, Miss Carlson, and Lil. "There's a long wide ledge. The lawn is six feet below that," he said. "Easy for handing down a stretcher."

Hart caught Lillian abruptly as she slumped, shocked out. Mike helped get her onto the bed and Miss Carlson fluttered over her.

"This is incredible!" muttered Lanis. "I can't understand it!"

"Then you'd better get a seeing-eye dog, Doctor," snapped Mike. "One of your patients is missing!"

∞

Five minutes later, Call Three went through to Washington for the second time in seven months. Senator Cain quietly convened another emergency session of the U.S. Senate Security Committee. A coded message also arrived minutes later in British Intelligence across the Atlantic. Somewhere under the Mojave Desert the miles' long installation known as the "Ranch" came alive, and red lights blinked on communication panels. In Northern California, far beneath the restful rustic lodge in the redwood grove, a special operator took up his station at a monitor screen. One more it was Omega Standby Condition Three. . . .

∞

John Anthony Hart shared the Olympian loneliness of presidents and kings. It was not a matter of choice; it was the inescapable price tag for what he had fallen into. Too much money, too much brilliance on the part of the staff he could buy. The technological breakthroughs were like nuclear power—far too big in their scope for private enterprise. He and his global organization were public property. Governments simply *had* to be involved. But even between the two entities— private and public power—the issues, all of the unknown quantities, and the apparent dangers, presented a magnitude of responsibility that overwhelmed. Neither Hart, nor his world integration of associated industrial-financial cartels, nor two major governments, felt that they were collectively ready.

So one tended to adopt the Machiavellian principle: one conscience for self, and one for the world. One could lie starkly staring at the ceiling in the privacy of one's own boudoir, tragically alone with what he *really* knew and feared or suspected; and yet one was forced to do lip service to the outer framework of normalcy, to the false interface one made with friends and loved ones. Mundane skepticism and the energetic reassurance of leadership. All pure bullshit, of course, but Black-Button mandatory. The facts and the terrors behind the masquerade—top secret.

Against the untenable part of it, to thwart the ghastly thrall of loneliness, to achieve a partnership in terror and splintered conscience, he had hoped for an ally in Dave Duqayne, as a successor and a son-in-law. But how could he tell him that the flunky vice-presidency in Credit-Mation Franchise Corporation was merely a camouflage for membership in the Lodge? A legit cover for an "O"-Man, an agent of

Omega. Mike was a second runner-up. He loved them both, as did Lillian, God bless her willowy hide! But before Mike could be brought on board, the subject of David Duqayne had to be resolved. He knew too much for the faceless opposition; he had been successfully operated on by a genius whom government Intelligence had fingered for entrapment, but the whole thing had boomeranged. Again, they had not been ready; and again his Machiavellian conscience was a kaleidoscope of brittle shards.

He and Brock had flown out to the "Ranch" in the Mojave so they could join a point-government conference on the carrier-scrambled TV satellite network. Cain chaired the meeting from the Committee Room in the Senate Building. The issue was Dave's disappearance, of course, but much, much more.

"This has gone too far," J.A. complained. "We let David play with the tiger when he wanted to set up his booby trap in the museum; he became the target and we couldn't protect him. Wishnow is dead and we can't even admit it. But now we're guilty of throwing Dave into double jeopardy."

"Dr. Borg was a valid choice to save him," retorted Senator Cain defensively. "At least according to Brock."

"As a surgeon, yes. But as to motivation, guess again!"

"We're convened here to do just that, J.A."

"You lost the trace on Borg," interjected Brockway. "We hadn't counted on that."

"Not to mention the loss of two more CIA," countered Cain, dourly. "But it *does* indicate the game we're playing."

"K-chromosomes? Rh-U blood types?"

"It would seem so."

Replete with Whitehall collar, rough tweeds and a waxed moustache, the British constituent of the Admiralty spoke up from MI-7, over in Trafalgar Square. There was the usual brittle commitment in his clipped tones. "Yes, well, be that as it may, gentlemen, we're chiefly concerned here with your security concerning *X*, you know."

"It's safe," said J.A. "Omega is green."

"Very good. In that case, all else is secondary, Mr. Hart."

"Gentlemen!" growled Hart. "I'm glad I can express myself personally about Dave Duqayne, since he's a definite key to the situation. In my book, his fate isn't secondary by a long shot! Now what I want to know is—where *are* we? Where do we go from here?"

"Caution, J.A.," warned Cain. "So far we've all been forced to walk on eggs in a surveillance mode. *Something* out there is very big, and without some sort of super weapon we'd be using Gatling guns against an armada of nuclear subs. At least until *X* proves itself."

The persistent British voice from the "blockhouse" on the Square chimed in again. "Perhaps a quick review. We have perceived so far—"

"That the K-chromosomes are getting ready to open up!" snapped Hart. "To hell with reviews. Let's decide the next step! Are there *any* new leads at all?"

"It would seem," said Cain, "that your boy Havelin is trying to help us out, but he can tip the applecart if he isn't restrained."

"What kind of a crack is that, Charlie?"

"I have a report here. Would he have any reason to be in your El Segundo plant last night around midnight?"

"Mike Havelin? No, I guess not. But at least it would be legal. He's part of our Security. What was he doing?"

"Having coffee with a certain night superintendant in Department 5-A."

"Hmm. The S-15 hydraulic line. No—can't figure it."

"You said he's a hound or a bulldog," remarked Brockway. "He *could* start chewing on the wrong throats—maybe an unnecessary irritant at this time."

"Well, dammit, he's sharp, and he's very close to me, like Dave."

"Too close," suggested Cain.

"All right! Then either I turn him on and make him a Lodge member, or I put him out to pasture in Ceylon or somewhere. He and my daughter are extremely up-tight right now. I can't keep the wool over their eyes forever."

"Gentlemen," said London, "when I suggested a review, I implied that we *did* have something new to add over here. . . ."

"Good, Leonard," said Cain. "By all means, let's have it."

The trans-Atlantic report was delivered succinctly, as unemotionally as a prescription for grandmother's dispepsia, in spite of the international magnitude of the subject, and in spite of the exotic technical equipment involved—satellites, code-scrambled carriers, voice-band FM multiplexing, and a monitored recording by the Bug. But in the middle of it, Hart's fingers started their telltale tapping. The stuff coming over *could* have a handle.

"The Swiss-based firm of *Allgemeine Penzberg-Hof A-G* is a cover name for something we have not quite determined. The name is obviously fictitious. . . ."

Brockway humphed and muttered restlessly into his empty pipe. Hart shushed him and the report went on. Not only were certain negotiations of the firm linked to the Mafia; one of their numbered accounts had been traced to a certain Sergius Thane, a mysterious international financial figure in some of the highest circles—but involving that kind of money which was known in the undergound as "dirty"; i.e., shrewdly illegal in that it was just barely beyond the reach of the law. Some of the information had leaked out through an intern at an exclusive sanitarium, known as Kronau.

"Wait a minute!" Hart cut in. The finger-tap cycle had reached its peak-out. "Mafia. That would tie in to the hit-and-run that was aimed at David. But as to motivation now. . . . High finances, yes, but *how?* How would Kettleridge and the K-Men be linked with Mafia, dirty money, and Dave?"

Brockway had been jawing his battered pipe stem while doodling intensively on a note pad. He shoved the pad over to Hart. Scrawled in his heavy hand with a red felt-tip pen was a short notation: *Allgemeine Penzberg H of A-G (=Aktiengesellschaft). . . . How about—ALPHA? Premeditated? ALPHA versus OMEGA!*

Hart shot him a look that said "maybe." The chin-cleft came into sudden prominence. He glared back intently at the London screen. "That sanitarium, Kronau. Isn't that the place that's famous for rejuvenation research?"

"We do have that as a matter of record."

"Hmm. Thane, Thane. . . . Was there a doctor mentioned by this intern? I mean, any doctor linked to treatments on Thane?"

During this, Cain and his committee had remained attentively silent, but Cain's expression revealed either an awakening interest or a growing impatience.

"Yes," replied London. "As a matter of fact, there was."

"I don't see where all of this is relevant," Cain broke in. "What we're mainly concerned with, J.A.—"

"No, wait, Charlie. I have a reason. What was the doctor's name?"

"There are several spellings available to us. Mail, and Mael. That's M-a-e-l. A Dr. Herman Mael."

Hart tensed toward the monitor screens. "Okay, gents, we have a breakthrough. That's it!" As Brockway and the transmitted countenance on the TV screens stared back wonderingly, he continued. "My hog-tied poor-man's Sherlock, Mike Havelin *does* get through after all, Charlie. He does a pretty good piece of legwork even under the handicap of being deliberately kept in the dark."

"I don't understand, J.A.," countered Cain. "Get to the point, if you please."

"His report on Dr. Jules Borg picked up an old alias, and it's right on the nose! *Herman Mael*, himself!"

"So?"

"It's an obvious lead! The underworld has some secret interest in the Kettleridge case, as shown by the hit-and-run on Dave, and by the way they got rid of Dr. Chafey in the middle of a supposed K-chromosome analysis. Now here's Thane, a top figure in shadow money and the Mafia—and Borg tied to Thane. I'd say our next move is a top-drawer override of the Fifth Amendment. You should start closing in on the local Cosa Nostra; somewhere, you should get a lead on Dave. If your boys need us, the Ranch, the Lodge, and the Bug are standing by. But I say, let's *move!*"

CHAPTER 5:
Gathering Storm

The darkness was void, and peace. . . .

Soft sweeping endlessness, adrift in a starless sea —the seventh sea of a world beyond Beyond. Galactic gulfs swallowed up like atoms in the gaping maw of emptiness never visited by Creation, waiting for Beginning that approached from a distance measured by forever.

Infinite dark nebulae billowing. . . . In the abyss of eons, a metallic echo: *duqayne . . . Duqayne . . . DUQAYNE!*

Ego evolves from primeval Limbo. The vibration of existence commences. The pendulum swings. The living clock ticks. A heart disembodied pulses, swirling through space, enhaloed by wobbling planets of blood. Mental winds shaking the pillars of Infinity. A blast of inner light. . . . The magic pinions and the wizard wheels . . . the silver cord not loosed, "nor the golden bowl not irreparably broken. . . ."

He lay in conscious darkness under gauze pads trying to remember—some mad dream about Dr. Borg and infant gods.

What do I care?

No voice spoke aloud, yet the thought was not his own.

The top man should be way up there—out of reach. . . .

For the first time in six months, Duqayne moved his limbs. His legs twitched. His fingers moved. He felt the bedcovers. But elation drowned in a wave of panic he couldn't define. Someone was speaking mentally. He was reading another's thoughts!

Nobody should know who he is. . . . You can't get away from "omerta."

Falteringly, trembling slightly, his hands raised

up and removed the bandages from his eyes. He lay in a luxurious bedroom and it was daylight outside with the blinds down, inviting soft-shadowed rest.

For ages without end!

This thought belonged to a second person. The impact of it was stronger, far more mature.

They have ruled us, but now perhaps we'll bring them to terms. . . . You've got to have a big club. . . . When the Gombah Capo gets too far away from his Family, maybe it's back to the mattress.

Where was he? What was happening to him? He was out of coma but terrorized by an experience to which he could not orient. His head felt strangely light as though his skull were ventilated. He raised up onto his elbows, then gingerly shook his head as though to clear it. This was a grave mistake. A momentary wave of nausea struck him when he *heard* the gush of blood through synthetic arteries. He vomited a spoonful of bitter bile, tightly grasping his bandaged cranium as though to squeeze away the dizziness.

God! what had Borg done to him? He had to find out, no matter what the cost. He stared at his strange, out-sized silken pajamas, then groped his way to his feet. Though basically weak, he seemed to be in command of a new reservoir of energy that pushed his body to obey. He staggered toward a pair of French doors nearby as though guided instinctively to the source of the mental emanations he had just received.

Through the venetian blinds he made out a flowered and terraced patio garden that yielded a high-altitude view of Hollywood and the smog-hazed Los Angeles basin. Somewhere in the Santa Monica hills. Bel Air? Brentwood? No. Too far east. This was directly above the Strip. One of those ultra-secluded mansions at the end of a high-curving road—the kind the tourists see from afar—a glimpse of floor-to-ceiling windows glinting aloft behind the cypresses in secret grandeur. One thing it spelled was money, if not power. But whose? Borg's? He doubted it because Borg seemed even more elusive—too surreptitious to be settled here even in the Olympian heights of the Establishment.

Seated comfortably on the near and higher split-level of the rambling Moorish terrace, their feet sprawled out on imported Italian tiles, were four men who helped themselves to drinks and hors d'oeuvre which had been placed before them on a lavishly inlaid coffee table. Two of them were obviously of Mediterranean blood, probably Italian; the kind the Syndicate would refer to as Guineas. They were garishly tailored and swarthy, with dark passionate lips, looking as though they wore shoulder holsters. A third man might well be the local proprietor inasmuch as he was more casually dressed and was the only one wearing open sandals. He was the tanned sportsman type, a crew-cut blond with sharp blue eyes under faintly tinted rimless glasses. He was middle-aged, in rugged physical trim; imposing, commanding, thin-lipped and cold. The fourth member of the party was Dr. Borg, hunched meditatively over his drink like a sentimental priest.

They were too far away for him to hear their conversation, yet he not only knew the inconsequential things they were saying aloud—he also caught their unexpressed thoughts even more clearly. He stared fixedly at them; incredulous, trembling, bathed in sweat.

The powerful mind of the proprietor spoke mentally again: *No guarantees here except the negative one—destruction. . . . There isn't any choice but to try. . . .*

One of the Syndicate types was also picked up: *For my dough, Thane could be one of them. Big enough to make Maranzano in his prime come on like a poor man's caporegime. Him being on our side is a trap!*

Then came a shocking bolt of superior mental power, from Borg himself: *Baboons, cobras, pigs, and spiders—how to control them? Only Duqayne. . . . Duqayne is the specific weapon of survival!*

Duqayne's mysterious energy reserve failed him. A hammer blow of vertigo changed the world suddenly, chuting him a thousand miles to the floor. And with him went the entire assembly of the venetian blinds, hangars and all, in a clatter loud enough to wake the dead. . . .

∞

Stars glittered through the glass panes of the undraped French doors. Indirect lighting illuminated the bedroom softly. Duqayne knew he was emerging from sedation. Borg sat there in a high-back chair by his bed and looked down at him with a stubborn patience.

"There now," he said, "that's more sensible, isn't it? *Calmly*, my boy! You are like a newborn child, unaware of your weaknesses or your strengths. You're going to have to accept my guidance through this critical period."

"Where am I?"

"Don't worry about it. You will know, all in good time."

"What have you done to my head? I feel strange."

"That is to be expected. However, in what way are you aware of this—ah—*strangeness*, as you say?"

"I heard voices!"

"Oh? What kind of voices?"

"They were thought voices—not what people were saying, but what they were *thinking*."

"Hmm. Very good! This is beyond what I had hoped for so soon. The experiment is a complete success. The most forbidden piece of surgical contraband in the universe. They said it couldn't be done." The doctor's dark eyes seemed to stare far off. There was a touch of triumph in his expression.

Duqayne struggled weakly onto his elbows. "Borg! I don't know what the hell kind of an animal *you* are, but I'm not a fucking guinea pig! For God's sake, don't tell me you actually did what you *said!*"

"What I said in the hospital? About wiring you?

Oh yes, Duqayne. You have new synthetic arteries, my boy, reaching deep into the cerebral cortex, and you have a conscious control of some of your glands, such as the adrenal. As a matter of fact, that's why you were able to get up on your feet at all!" He absorbed Duqayne's threatening stare with pleasant equanimity. "The effect will be cumulative and rapid; rather exponential, I'd say."

"You dirty, filthy—"

"Oh calm down now, and use that brain more effectively, Duqayne. You would have died. I brought you back and gave you a new incarnation—a veritable godling with the mental wings of a Prometheus. You've only begun to awaken to your new capabilities."

Duqayne dropped back to his pillow. "I can't believe it! But if it's true, then *why?* You say I was fingered for death."

Borg's vague smile wiped off to a cold frown. "You still are, unless you do exactly what I tell you to do. . . ."

There was a waiting silence between the two of them. It was a time when one notices the shape and texture of another's eyes. Borg's small black eyes were not corner-crinkled with amusement or kindness. They were eyes bigger than life but set tightly in a plastic mask, unfeatured except for the smouldering fire in their abysmal depths. But if this surgical madman had really given him a contraband gift of the gods, perhaps it could be made to boomerang. He groped inward mentally, striving to collect his mental powers. He felt a focusing of awareness in his frontal lobes, sensed a capability of concentration he had never known before.

"Okay, Dr. Frankenstein," he taunted, "but what if the monster breaks loose?"

Borg's strange eyes narrowed, but their intensity brightened. "It would be very interesting to have you try that. Very interesting. As a matter of fact, you are trying to probe into my mind now. Go ahead,

Duqayne—try hard! You must flex your new muscles, you know. Doctor's orders!"

I'm crazy, thought Duqayne. This isn't happening—I should be dead. It's a dream—a nightmare. But what the hell do I do? Concentrate! If you've got the goddam moxie, then *throw* it at the son of a bitch!

Feeling much like Kafka's cockroach, he flexed unaccustomed limbs—strange new extensions of the mind. The mind-force seemed to pack itself into a third eye, as it were, somewhere behind and between his brows. Like a bullet he launched the intangible probe, willing a vision of Borg's private thoughts behind that tonsured cranium—and became aware of a granite wall. Blocked!

"Are you such a fool, Duqayne? How could I play the most dangerous game in the world without self-protection? The mahout has his elephant pick, the tiger tamer his whip! In mathematical terms, my friend, the truth table of variables has been reduced to the minimum equation!"

Duqayne sweated. Conscious control of the adrenals? Okay, pour it on! With a newly awakened instinct, he gathered psychic forces from the power centers in his back, from vast neural reservoirs of the solar plexus, from behind the pineal, and from a lurking mystery-power that seemed to reside on *top* of his head. He felt the new compaction, a charged force that waited for the trigger of his will—and he fired it.

The granite wall wavered momentarily, then slowly began to recede and attenuate, giving a hint of *prepared* darkness, the swirling mists roiling restlessly.

Telepathically, Borg's powerful thought registered clearly: *You once caught a glimpse of an alien, and you almost failed to recover. You didn't know that I, too, have seen our slave masters, and in my mind is their image, Duqayne. . . . Behold!*

A long dark corridor, his point-of-view racing down it toward a massive door of Babylonian design and stained with age. The door swung back ponderously into half darkness. An impression of cavernous depths and a giant figure looming, misted in a stench of the living dead. The putrescent face again, the ancient anguish, the threat of monster hate and destruction. . . .

Duqayne threw a hand across his eyes and yelled hoarsely in a paroxysm of pain and horror. . . .

∞

The usual posh perfection of the penthouse was in considerable disarray. Empty coffee cups, filled ashtrays, reports, discarded newspapers—and a flat haze of smoke from Mike's pipe drifting near the ceiling as though on an inversion layer. Hart was on the phone, his brown coat removed, cufflinks gone, sleeves turned back. Doodle pads and pencils were in profusion, plus tape cassets for phone recordings; the recorder itself in a welter of wires, crumpled paper and half-empty drink glasses. The glazed remains of paper-dish catered suppers were shoved to one side. Stanley Pagem, Hart's No. 1 Black Button male secretary, had been told to stay with them and to throw away the clock—even the calendar. A slight, very lean and neat young man with an almost non-Establishment mass of dark blond hair, he sat on a sofa in blue pin-striped shirt, squinting through cigarette smoke and carefully reviewing a thick sheaf of reports on an oversized clipboard.

Hart hung up the phone, glared at Mike and Pagem, then flipped the rewind on the recorder. "Maybe you heard my side of the conversation," he said. "You might as well get it all. And Mike, we're cracking your chastity belt tonight. Just make like you're top secret. Nothing beyond this room, okay?"

Mike didn't smile. He only reloaded his trusty briar for continued heavy duty. In fact, he frowned slightly as though to imply that it was high time Hart leveled with him.

Hart flipped that "play" switch. "This is Undersecretary Connolly, L.A. Federal Building. Liaison between the State and Justice Departments, the FBI, and the CIA. Direct line, scrambled and decoded. Now listen!"

Mike sat back and listened while Pagem made notes, although he wondered why that was necessary with a recording. Maybe a habit with the executive aide types, he reflected. He stared up through a fresh cloud of pipe smoke at the acoustic ceiling, relaxing his body and marshaling his mind to absorb every word. Looking at him, one might have thought he was half asleep and listening to a recorded concert.

The "concert" played on, developing for Mike an elaborate tapestry of events and circumstances which he had long suspected but hardly dared to believe. Where much of it was new to his experience, it only served to aggravate the persistent itch-worms in the marrow of his stubborn personality.

The first part of the recording dealt with secret local forays into some of the local "Family" strongholds of the Syndicate. No direct lead to Dave or Dr. Borg had been uncovered, as yet, but certain other revelations were, to the State Department, of much heavier import.

A new pattern was creeping into the almost century-old modus operandi of the local Syndicate boys. They were following the modern trend of mergering, but apparently it had nothing to do with stock leverages or antitrust. By "merger" was meant an unprecedented new affiliation with the underground power structures—the Jewish *and* the Middle East combines, including the whole shadow-money logjam behind frozen Euro-Dollars—that phantom world-echelon of finance that orbited serenely above the system of banks, insurance companies, mutual funds, Federal Reserve, and the World Bank. This combine could control hundreds of billions and topple empires. Fortunately, Wall Street, Fleet Street, Paris, Istanbul, and Beirut were not yet in on the "know," as otherwise the speculation might produce a panic.

"Of course we have Merchants and Manufacturers, plus Chemical Trust and others on our neck, but they're all counting on you and the Lodge," commented the undersecretary cautiously. "They've picked up a whiff of this situation and we have to fend them off. No panic, using your name, but they have never heard of Omega, of course."

Mike cast a glance at Hart, who gave him a blank look. So the cat in the bag was tiger-sized, after all, he thought. The wily little bastard was in some kind of a box, unable to level even with his own mother. J.A. was obviously forced to wear several faces around here, and it was becoming a Devil's Mardi Gras.

The little tape casette continued to unwind. The total armament was far more formidable and effective than nuclear politics. It was dollars, not missiles. And with dollars you could buy Man's soul. After all, the real battle of the Civil War had been behind the scenes in Europe; the struggle for Union credit, between cotton-backed Confederate dollars and Lincoln's gold "green-back" gamble. *This*, however, was far more global in its nature. What were they after? What was the scare?

"We have reason to believe it's happening," conceded the undersecretary. "The entire rationale behind the Kettleridge affair has been borne out completely, J.A. This isn't official yet, and Cain is holding it down, but I can tell you that Duqayne was right all along. What we only dared to suspect back in '62 was valid. The K-Men exist. We're being tapped. They *are* emerging. Money is a major weapon and they're out to get Omega."

Hart's filtered voice cut in on the tape recording. "What you're really saying is, they want *X*."

"Our policy there," replied the undersecretary grimly, "would be war—not against another government —but war. You know what I mean. Both the resources of the United States, the British Government, and of course Omega would then be committed. After all, the exposure to telepathic espionage is crisis enough—but the theft of X would be strictly Condition One."

"Would you say that the Syndicate and their foreign affiliates are under the control of the K-Faction?" Hart was heard to ask.

"Well, we've reviewed the report you heard yesterday from MI-7. What is your opinion of Thane and the *Allgemeine Penzberg-Hof A-G?*"

"Brockway thought it might spell *Alpha.* I forgot to pass that on."

"Alpha! Hmm. Alpha versus Omega. It *could* have significance. Incidentally, what helps to ring the panic button is a general picture of big meetings all over— Zurich, Jamaica, Cuba, Miami, Vegas, L.A. The expatriates are floating in from Sicily. It's like *Walpurgisnacht* on the Mountain. Something of historical proportions is brewing. We suggest that you keep the 'Ranch' on 24-hour status."

"It always is."

"Okay. Then the other recommendation is to get up to the Lodge. Maximum security. We'll provide you with extra personnel."

"Is the Pentagon in on this yet?"

"Joint Chiefs only; certainly not *all* of the Cabinet. This is Presidential level. Only Cain and his committee are cognizant, plus the Secretary and myself. And of course, specially processed members of Justice, the CIA, and a few FBI. It's more top secret than the Manhattan Project."

The report tapered off into amenities, including an inquiry about Lillian.

"No change," Hart's voice replied. "She's still under sedatives. Nasty shock, poor kid!"

When it ended, Hart clicked off the recorder and stared at Mike, who got up and hotly paced the floor. No. 1 watched him curiously. Finally, he turned to Hart with a full head of steam.

"Thank *you,* J.A., for all the enlightenment! I can appreciate the magnitude of the State Department's concern. It's all incredible and it *could* scare the shit out of Congress, if they knew. But what about Dave? I'm only human, a goddam little ex-private dick lost in the great big shuffle! He *is* one of the major keys to the situation. What's the plan on him and Borg?"

Hart shrugged. "Everybody's working on it. Do you have any suggestions?"

"Yes! I'll go it alone!"

"Don't be an idiot! This is bigger than all of us!"

"So? That's what they'll be looking for—a big operation. But when the scene gets *too* big, you lose sight of the little things such as the former operations of Duqayne-Havelin Associates, b.K.—that's 'before Kettleridge.' After all, Dave and I weren't exactly wet behind the ears in our business, J.A. We had our informers, we knew the gutter grapevines. The damn Syndicate isn't *that* invisible! I still remember a few side names—you know, payoff men, borderliners, the interface operators."

"The heat's too high, Mike. You'd go down in flames before you got started. As a matter of fact, I have other plans for you. How about coming up to the Lodge with me?"

No. 1 seemed to be deeply impressed by this suggestion. Whatever the "Lodge" might be, it obviously signified a flattering promotion into the Black Button fraternity.

"I can't tell you why just now, Mike, but I stuck my neck out letting you hear this tape. I took the liberty of committing you to my plans."

"*Why*, John?"

"Damn it! Because you're Dave's buddy and you've been in love with Lillian all your life. You're not about to toss your marbles at a time like this!"

"How right you are, John, all the way!"

"Besides that, you're an ex-Marine commando and CIA man; loyal, hard as rocks, and practical. Now what's your pitch, Mike? You've got something on your mind."

"Sure I have, but you and Cain refuse to buy it. It's Brockway. I think he's Mr. Big—behind it all!"

"Bull! You take my word, Mike. Don't waste your time."

"Okay, I won't. I'll just nurse it along by myself. I gave you an alias for Borg, but the payoff will be when I can tie the name of *Thane* to Irving Brockway. . . ."

There was a mutual eye-lock and a pall of silence. Hart glanced at No. 1 significantly. The bright young man waved his clipboard and headed for the business section of the rooftop suite. "I'll be in Xerox," he said.

When he had gone, J.A. mixed himself a drink at the bar, which was not his habit. "Mike, you've got me between a rock and a hard spot, just as Dave did before he got hit. You know why we kept holding him back? Because we weren't ready. Both of you are bulldogs and you can tear the wrong pants at the wrong time. But I needed Dave in a way I couldn't explain. He didn't want that job in Credit-Mation, and I couldn't tell him it was a front for something else. Now I'm making passes at *you* and you don't get it either!"

"Maybe neither one of us is much good with the double-talk." Mike regretted his phraseology as the old man's eyes flared up. "I don't mean it that way, J.A. I just mean, why can't you simply lay it on the line?"

"If I could, I would. You know too much already."

"What—the Lodge? The Bug? The Ranch? Omega and *X*? Hell, it's all Greek to me!"

"But it's all top secret, and you know security regulations enough to realize—"

"Sure! Either shoot me or join me up! It's as simple as that, isn't it?"

"Not quite. When you cross the line into Omega, your life won't be your own any more."

Mike studied the tycoon's leathery pinched face. It looked forlorn, weary; the famous zap shot out of it for the moment. "Is your life *your* own?" he asked.

"No."

"I figured as much."

"I'm a lonely man, Mike. Too much for one pair of shoulders, and mine aren't getting any broader."

"Okay, so you had Dave picked for a son-in-law, and now that you're not sure—"

"We'll find him," snapped Hart, coming alive again. "Don't be shitty, Mike, goddam it! I want you both!"

Mike made himself a drink. Both men were close beside each other behind the bar, leaning on it with their most private thoughts teetering for a spill. It was an odd time. It was the best time.

"Okay," Mike started. "I gather something bigger than Hitler is turning on, and somehow you've gotten yourself committed. I know the Kettleridge bit, I've read Dave's article, hashed it out with both him and Lil—I *saw* what happened to Dr. Chafey. K-chromosome types, mental mutants—the whole shmear. I can see the implications. Even governments wouldn't know which ally to confide in or whom to trust. And you sure as hell can't let a thing like this get on TV! It has enough panic-potential to collapse the stock market over night. People wouldn't be working; they'd be walking in the streets or heading for the hills. I gather this X you're talking about is a super-weapon or something, and you're all fighting for time; but the K-Men are moving too fast. I also gather that these K-Men don't pack heavy numbers. They need an extension of themselves, so they've tied in the underground syndicates on a global scale. But that leads to something else. Goons, gombahs, top shylocks in the international crime cartels. They're either too dumb or too smart to swallow anything like the K-Men, and no matter if you scared their pants off they wouldn't knuckle under. They're just not constituted to recognize a power greater than their own. Therefore, I'll lay you odds they don't know who Mr. Big is, either, but they're being given the biggest come-on in the history of the world. And there's only one thing bigger than a slice of el dopo, the numbers, prostitution, protection, and world cartel controls. And they're drooling for it."

Hart scanned Mike's hard face with fatherly appreciation. "You're hot so far, Sherlock. You ought to be able to name it."

"It's X isn't it?"

"Yup!"

"And you can't tell me what it is."

"Not yet, unless—"

"Hold it. There's another thing. I caught that jargon about Alpha and Omega. If Alpha controls hundreds of billions of dollars, that's like half the money in the world. What's Omega got?"

"The other half."

"What?"

"Omega is a facetious but effective acronym, Mike. Somebody was kidding around when they came up with it. But nothing fits better. It means: 'Organization of Megamillions Anonymous.'"

Mike took a deep slug of his drink. After a long, tense and staring silence: "I can see what one of our great financiers meant when he made the crack that if people knew the facts behind money, there'd be blood in the streets!"

"There can be *worse* things than blood-letting, Mike." Hart turned to him earnestly. "Now what I started to tell you—"

"No, J.A. I've got an instinct about this. Thanks, but leave me out for a while."

"I'm asking you to join me, Mike. It's lonely as hell up here!"

"You're damn right it is! Things are tough all over! It's a bad alley, J.A.—dark as the Pit. But somewhere in there is a lonely cat named Dave Duqayne. You know an army makes a big clatter in a place like that. I'm laying you odds that a broken-down gum-shoe like me can cast less of a shadow and tip over fewer garbage cans."

Hart's expression hardened. "Oh for God's sake, Mike! What do you think gives *you* the odds over all of us?"

"I'm a lot more anonymous than Omega—to *Them*, that is. As a nobody coming from left field, my mask is as good as the Devil's."

"You're a fool!"

"Can you stop me?"

"Yes."

"Will you?"

"No."

"If I yell for help, can I have it?"

"The works. But Cain's concern is that you might get in the way."

"I understand the consequences. That's why I won't."

"Mike, what were you doing the other night in Department 5-A?"

"Oh that! I forgot to mention it. Your crack the other night about vulcanizing on the S-15 line made me curious. They're not running that operation on Swing. . . ."

"So?"

"So you must have imagined it."

"Imagined what?"

"The smell of sulphur. . . ."

CHAPTER 6:
To Catch a Demon

For Lillian Hart, the Kettleridge case had burdened her instinct with a fear that was disturbingly atavistic. In mental defense she had rejected David's conclusions on the surface; but beneath it all, she had never been able to dodge the brute force of its horrible implications. Seen dimly behind Genesis 6:4 and the K-chromosome theory was the dreaded veil, a mist of encroaching darkness like the greenish vapor surrounding the elemental creature she had once seen. A threat of soul destruction, a fulfillment of the forbidden ancient knowledge that a benevolent Providence had sought to wash from the Earth in cataclysmic flood. A fragment had survived. It was emerging again. A malignance superior to human evil was abroad in the world.

David's and her father's mention of a "new model of the universe" had only made it all the more terrifying. Since the emergence of the K-Man theory, they had said, scientists who knew about it were looking into "bio-plasma" and other formerly *psi* phenomena in terms of higher energy states; or *actual* planes of existence lying beyond the normal ranges of human perception. According to this disturbing concept, they say, *nothing* was supernatural, whether one referred to demigods or demons. Therefore, many phenomena formerly relegated to witchcraft, alchemy, spiritualism, or pure superstition might well be signs of a *physical* reality. In other words, it was like bringing to life the old science-fiction concept of other dimensions, or "parallel universes." The very threat of such a model of the universe at once dissolved the rapture of fantasizing, and left one staring inwardly as though facing the Dweller on the Threshold.

No wonder, she thought, that such a panic level of

secrecy was involved. If the general public were to hear about it—or even faintly comprehend its cosmic import—the result could only be chaos. In spite of all her own extensive knowledge and training in such esoterica, it was all she could do to keep from becoming irrational.

Then had come the inscrutable Irving Brockway, a man one watched from the corner of an eye because elsewhere or else-when he could assume another shape. Fear fancy, perhaps, or instinct jitters, yet the metaphor was weirdly satisfying. After the museum episode, however, and Dave's prophetic claim of being a target—and after he had actually been struck down in the wake of Dr. Chafey's death—the shape of Brockway in the corner of her eye had become more menacing, though still amorphous. Was it Mike convincing her on the basis of deduction, or her convincing *him* on a paragnostic level? Whatever it was, it had compounded itself with the mysterious advent of Dr. Borg.

This had been too much. The shock of Dave's tragedy at the brink of marriage, the long-drawn agony of witnessing his helpless suffering—then the sudden thin hope of a breakthrough only to be followed by his sinister disappearance. Not to mention the discovery that Mike was as much in love with her as ever, and now obviously twice damned himself for revealing it to her at such an ill-timed moment.

So, inevitably, a nervous breakdown, and now dazed recovery. The aftereffects of her traumatic siege had taken the form of a moral lethargy that deprived her of the will to find her legs again. She would lie in bed for hours and stare at the ceiling in broad daylight, unaware of anything but a pent-up scream gathering in her, a cry of soul pain that rattled the barriers of sedation.

On the other hand she knew that such a blanking of consciousness was the true psychic state; a threshold condition that exposed her directly to the subconscious, which in her case could be dangerous.

Deliberately she nursed an awakening tendency to wool gather. At times, dream-borderland fantasies would drift before her mental eye, mingling color, sound and thought-image in a sort of liquid 3-D kaleidoscope of surrealistic impressions. But in their midst a disturbing new consistency emerged—astrological symbols . . . Aries the Ram. The rising Saturnine goat-face bothered her, and once in nightmarish warning it assumed the features of Dr. Brockway. It spoke to her balefully, saying: "Long before the sunrise, child. The sheep were asleep in the meadow."

Aries . . . Ram . . . the male of the sheep. Sunrise? The Vernal Equinox, the sun sign. A terrible meaning there, struggling to rise to the surface but held from her as though forbidden. Why had Brockway spoken in parable? She could have sworn he was toying with her intellect from some superhuman stratosphere.

A tingling touched her. An inner stillness fell upon her like sudden night or as in the eclipse of light by vast wings. A moment of unexplained nightmare. In a chilling thrill of terror she knew she had been gripped by some mesmeric state, a psychic eddy, imperceptible at first because of its wide-wheeling current, now locking her in its spiral and pulling her inexorably toward its funneling darknesses.

Her morbid thought associations had brought her to a malefic frame of mind. In her weakness of will, the subliminal imagery transplanted her in time and space to the focal point of her most defiling spiritual adventure—the coven seance with Cyprian and Melusina. In some inexplicable euphoria of evil, the group had challenged priest and priestess to deepen the mystique of their power, to prove that their subphyches could survive the terrors of a forbidden "step beyond" into the supreme atavism of the Universal Id.

It had happened then, and to her abysmal horror it was happening now, here in her bedroom where she was alone and unprotected by her athamé or burning thurible or circling symbols and amulets. She hadn't even the will to reach for her necklace in the drawer of her night stand. A psychic dimming encroached; a greenish mist materialized like a stagnant breath from slime-locked swamps. It was like a conjured attack, yet she knew of no mental enemy but herself. She hadn't ever made the final commitment of witchcraft or developed a protective familiar; there were no clever, demonic *magistelli* now to fend off this horror that approached her. The mists thickened, and into their swirling convolutions of color and shadow crept the looming outlines of a monstrous face. . . .

She tried to envision mental symbols to shield her —the cross of Rowan, the hexagrams, the pentagram of Solomon. She feebly incanted the countering spells; half-forgotten words without the will to drive them into a cone of force. "Pentacle of Power, be thou fortress and defense—"

A hint of beetling wolf-brow and burning eyes, a gleam of slavering needle fangs. There was a stench of mindless lust, a threat of soul-rending, a doom of madness.

"By Barabbas!" she cried out, perspiring in terror. "By Satanas, by the devil cursed be!"

The Id monster drifted from curtains of fantasy and was there, materialized above her. Her mind reeled. She screamed the only name left to her spiritual inventory—one she had not known was so deep a part of her inner levels.

"David! *David!*—for the love of God!"

As though a bridge were spanned, like a sudden bolt of power, a *wind* of force smashed through the whirlpool of mental mists. A bestial snarling rent her ears—a roaring that receded. The monster eyes faded back into the primeval Limbo, and the darkness slowly lifted.

I am here. . . .

Her breath and her pulse seemed to stop. Time halted for some measureless period while she took desperate sensory inventory. Had she heard a voice reply, or was it dream hypnosis induced by her terrible need for strength and help?

"David?" She half-whispered his name and dared to look about her. The drapes were drawn but sunlight filtered through sufficiently to reveal the contents of the wide, luxuriously furnished bedroom. It was empty.

Don't panic, Lil. I'm here with you. . . .

She sat bolt upright in bed and shook her head frenziedly to clear it.

No, you are not losing your mind, Lillian. I swear I am here. You are having a telepathic experience.

True, the voice was mental, not audible, but it was too much for emotional control or immediate comprehension. In spite of her intimate rapport with the *man*, David Duqayne, in his disembodied presence her flesh crawled. "Oh Dave, forgive me—I can't—!"

Don't get the wrong idea, Lil. I am not dead—not yet.

"Then for the love of God, where *are* you! You say you're here, darling. *Show* yourself!"

Perhaps it's too much for now. I can come back. . . .

"No! If you go away now I *know* I'll lose my mind —but I've got to look at you!"

Only if you calm yourself. . . .

"Yes, yes—I promise!"

Suddenly he was there, in green silk pajamas and a bandaged head. He sat in the arm chair by the reading lamp not eight feet away, staring at her solemnly as she caught her breath sharply and bit her lower lip to stifle a scream. It was an astral image, ghostly, white, faintly transparent.

"Pray God I'm only delirious! Are you—" She moved as though to get out of bed, unheedful of her revealing dishabille. "Oh Dave, darling, Dave—!"

"Stay there, Lil . . . don't move."

She thought she heard his voice audibly now, yet somehow it seemed to be muted by an invisible barrier.

"You must take my word for it—you're not looking at a ghost. I'm quite alive. You've heard they do this stuff in Tibet—you often told me about it yourself and you believed it. Well, here it is. I'm not here physically . . . or who knows what 'physical' is anymore? The lid's blown off of whatever we knew before. . . ."

"But, I don't understand. . . . After the operation, you—"

"Later, Lil. I haven't much time. I want you to listen to me. But first I have to scold you—seriously. Why in hell didn't you tell me how dangerously involved you were with forces you shouldn't *ever* play with? That *thing* that was here—"

"I know, I know, but David—!"

"It was stark, sheer terror that saved you. It helped me bridge over. I was trying to reach you—you called me through."

"And you exorcised it. How—?"

"Never mind—just listen. That materialization you had was real enough, but child's play compared to what's *really* going on. The thing I just blasted out of here was what I believe you call an elemental— a manifestation of some lower dimension of the astral. What *I'm* involved with is on a much closer psychic level, a conscious and super-intelligent evil that can massively destroy or enslave. Everything I suspected is true. An alien breed of mental monstrosities walks the Earth. They are capable of masquerading as humans; friend, relative, financier, world leader— *anybody!*"

"David, whatever it is—whatever you say—all right! But where *are* you? Where can I go to find you?"

"Maybe it's better that you *never* find me. That's what I came to tell you."

"You can't possibly mean what you're saying!"

"I think I'm going to have to mean it."

"You can't *do* this to me! I won't let you!"

"The operation did it, Lil. Dr. Borg works for *them,* and the aliens—and so does the underworld, unsuspectingly. Those who *know* what's going on, like

Borg—well, some of them are in a kind of revolt. They, or at least Borg, have need of a counterweapon, and that's what he thinks he's created in *me*. One way or another, my life is forfeited, Lillian. I want you to marry Mike and forget me."

She began to bawl, just staring at him with the tears running down her face. He could read the hurt in her mind. He heard the soul cry—desolation, fear, inability to cope. There wasn't much of that he could take. He had to get through, and fast. His strength would soon run out.

"Borg didn't leave me a man, Lil. I'm something else, with synthetic arteries and voluntary endocrines —wired for sound, baby. You wouldn't want to take *that* to bed with you. I'm a freak!"

"No you're not, Dave! You're not! Please don't!" The words were swift, softly spoken in monotone. The tears said more.

"I have work to do—don't you see that? If what's left of me has a built-in compensating factor, then I've got to use it. Your father would understand—so would Mike. And if they were sensitives like you I'd be talking to them now. I will later, when I'm stronger. But there are no more personal considerations. They tore my pink slip, honey. I'm no longer Dave Duqayne . . . this is Superweapon Number One speaking."

"Oh, Dave! Dave!" She swung her softly tanned legs out of the bed and got up and ran to him with outflung arms, her sheer half-nightie embellishing her nymph-like nudity.

He disappeared from the chair but then reappeared in the middle of the room, glaring at her. She felt the suffocating impact of huge mental power. Sobbing, she huddled in the chair watching him and she trembled at the sudden strangeness of him. Yet a shred of character strength made her fight back. "David I swear—if you do this to us—if you withdraw into this demon wizardry, whatever it is—I'll *join* you!"

"You'll join me *how?*" he demanded angrily.

"So help me, I'll make the commitment. I'll cross the line with Cyprian and Melusina. I'll follow you on *whatever* plane!"

"No! Your witchcraft is silly and dangerous dabbling. I forbid it, do you hear?"

"Then don't threaten me with separation!"

"It's not a threat—it's fact. I'm a monster, don't you get it? Or perhaps I should demonstrate, to break you off once and for all. Fight fire with fire, Lillian. To catch a demon, *be* one!" His image hurtled at her from a vast distance, becoming infinite, leaving only the hypnotic dark eyes. "If it's the honeymoon you wanted, we can get it over with, Lillian. How about *this* one?"

She felt herself swept away into a maelstrom. Swirling stars and nebulae . . . boiling suns . . . million-mile coronas spewing forth the magma sperm of stellar regeneration. . . .

From heart and hearth of the human clay, fly with me, lover! Ride a meteor of madness into the cauldron of Creation. Fill your eyes, beloved, and your mind and your soul, with the insupportable rapture and despair of total Cosmic perspective!

She hurtled through writhing galaxies in horrendous collision, her senses violated by sounds and color and brilliance beyond endurance. Screaming in vertigo, she plummeted at last mercifully into oblivion, her psyche shorted by a god-bolt of untenable revelation. . . .

∞

Bastard! Bastard! He yelled the epithet silently while struggling through a cloying white fog that roared like a cataract in his ears. He didn't have to be so rough with her, but she drove him out of his mind with her own inimitable essence. Woman essence, yet soft and girlish in tearful disarray, hugging her smooth thighs and her shining knees in the arm chair, the dark bower of her hair a goddess glade in which he saw her injured spirit trembling and ready to die. He couldn't have it. Shock treatment was the only way out—she *had* to forget him! Mike was the only answer. But the pain of hurting her cut bloody scars, claw-mark gutters that gushed a new acid of hate—a monster-hate to compensate for everything that had been taken away. . . .

The fog attenuated, revealing an anaesthetic gas hood. Above it frowned Dr. Borg, who held the apparatus firmly in place.

"You're reaching out too fast and too far, Duqayne. I don't trust you! So now you will sleep for a while. And when you awaken—"

Duqayne grasped the doctor's burly arms. He struggled. Somewhere in the lighted bedroom there were menacing voices.

"Hey! You got troubles, Doc?"

Still struggling to hold the mask in place. Borg shouted at them. "Get out of here, you fools! Don't interfere!"

The distraction was sufficient. Duqayne knocked the gas hood aside and shot a mental bolt into Borg's widened eyes. The bearded surgeon recoiled, momentarily grasping his temples in pain. The two Mafia types, seen earlier on the patio terrace, loomed behind him, dark Latin faces scowling suspiciously in sudden alarm as Duqayne raised up in bed.

"Get out!" shouted Borg. "Get out for your lives!"

"Hey, I don't like this, Doc! So what's the rumble here, hah?"

Behind the two Syndicate members, the crew-cut blond sportsman now stepped quietly into the room and assessed the situation coldly. He remained aloof and expressionless as Borg pushed the two thugs back from the bed.

"I told you he's dangerous!" Borg insisted angrily. "Now get out! And don't get trigger-happy! He's absolutely priceless to us. Just let *me* handle him!"

The shorter and more swarthy of the two gave Borg a shove and followed it up with a vicious slap.

A gun appeared in his hand. *"Nobody* bosses me, you get it!? Just get that straight, Doc, okay? Now look! I didn't pull in the *capos* from three continents just to sit under a lid and wait for *you* to lift it!" He slapped his chest heatedly. "This is Cosa Nostra! When we ask what's going on, that's what we want you should tell us! We waited long enough, okay?"

During this, Duqayne remained propped on his elbows glaring intently at everyone in the room. In addition to the audible din of argument, the mental atmosphere was a flak-burst of rattled thoughts— hate, greed, ego resentment, suspicion, the cold-blooded threat of murder. But from two sources came an underlying tide of steadier thought, massively mature. One source was Borg, whose alarm was purposeful and urgent. His mind was on the gas generator and the instant need for putting Duqayne under restraint. The other source was their host, who had a weirdly frightening propensity for translating every circumstance into a monetary evaluation. An international financier, his emotions had apparently been traded for dollars. He toyed with thoughts of mercy or assassination purely in the form of a balance sheet in *twelve* figures. . . .

The second Syndicate member was complaining. "Yeah, we only went for all this secret bullshit because Mr. Big wants a meeting. So don't try to run this show, Doc. It's too big even for *you!*"

"Shut up!" The financier produced a black cheroot and proceeded to light it as if he had spoken to puppies. "It's too big for *all* of you! Borg, you'd better handle this or you know who will. The stakes are too high for any deviations—none at all, from any of us. Do you understand?"

The gun-wielding member sneered. "Listen, Blue Chip, you're only the bankroll *consigliere,* not the Boss. Go buy yourself a couple of corporations, but just keep out of our way!"

Blue Chip drew easily on the cheroot. "I don't deal in cigar stands. You know what I represent. If our kind don't keep the calf fatted, your kind runs out of carrion. We've both got to put the tiger in his cage. . . ."

"Tiger, shmiger! I've had it with your bogeyman! You got a big lip—now I'll give it to you straight—!" The gunman moved swiftly to the bed and pressed the muzzle of his weapon against Duqayne's bandaged head. "One minute, Borg." He checked his wrist-watch. "Gimme the lowdown on this stupid guinea pig, right now! Or he gets a new hole in his head!"

His companion joined him, also brandishing his gun—a snub-nosed .38. "That's right, Doc. What makes Duqayne the key to a worldwide setup? I know we got threats. All these goons nobody sees and only Mr. Big can handle, but—" He nodded toward Duqayne. "So what's with Hot Stuff? What's he got? Come on, come on, *give!*"

"Your time's running out, Doc." The man with the gun at Dave's head again checked his watch.

Borg and the financier exchanged glances. The latter was calmly quizzical, squinting through a thin haze of smoke. On Borg's pasty but scholarly counten-ance appeared a thin, egotistical smile. He turned to assess Duqayne's mood cautiously.

"Thirty seconds, Doc," announced the gunman.

Duqayne methodically gathered every shred of psychic energy, sensing a pull even from his guts, up his spine, out of the visceral centers, from behind his throat and pineal—and again from that mysterious aura hovering beyond his cranium. He slowly cen-tered a bolt of devastation at what seemed to be the focal point of the will, between his eyes.

Borg knew it. He covertly encouraged it. *Hold your fire, Duqayne.* The mental message was calm, crisp, compelling. *Follow my cue!*

"I think," said Borg aloud, "that the patient him-self can accommodate you." As all eyes turned to Duqayne, he added, "How about it, Duqayne? Your life is at stake. The man wants an answer. . . ."

This was followed by an urgent telepathic signal:

Now! Give it all you've got!

Gleaming with sweat, Duqayne turned to look above and beyond the gun muzzle directly into the gunman's eyes. In that instant, each person in the room felt a psychic wind pass through him like a silent shock wave, but its force was focused on the gunman. He screamed in agony, dropping the gun and grabbing his temples. In blind terror, he ran from the room.

The second gunman backed away like a man staring at an onrushing locomotive. "I'm getting out of here!" he yelled. Forgetting the weapon in his hand, he precipitately followed his companion.

"That was smart, Borg," commented Blue Chip. "Now get smarter and put your boy under control." As he noted Duqayne's tense, threatening stare, he addressed him directly. "As for you—" He deliberately savored his cheroot. "I guess you know the score, what we are, and what we're fighting. If you don't like it, just remember this thing is the great granddaddy of Death and Taxes—so don't play Jesus." He turned to leave, but at the door he spoke to Borg. "I just got off the phone. Thane is ready. The meeting is tomorrow." With a significant gaze, he closed the door.

From the financier's mind, Duqayne caught a thought-image of something shadowy, vast; a distant entity of superhuman stature. It was related to the secret name of *Thane*. Even more startling was the fact that the closing of the door effectively cut off the mental impression.

"*I* blocked that," said Borg. "You'll know what you're supposed to know when I want you to know it."

Duqayne sank back weakly onto his pillow. He had been through too much. He had drained himself physically, psychically, emotionally. Borg came to the bed and looked down at him triumphantly.

"The adrenalin finally gave out, did it? I *thought* I gave you enough gas. That was close, Duqayne. You will never get a chance again to use that mind of yours against me—or against *anyone*, unless I tell

105

you when to use it and how. . . ."

Duqayne was helpless to respond in any manner. He could only lie there and watch his captor with heavy-lidded eyes, all but devoid of thought.

Borg sat down on the bed, the caricature of a solicitous father. He tucked him in deftly. "You will listen now to my voice, Duqayne . . . and you will do what I tell you to do. You have no other choice, because you are sinking into a special kind of sleep —just enough hallucinogens to soften your ego *and* your will. . . ."

Duqayne's eyelids were iron trapdoors settling heavily. A blanketing darkness gripped him. Dr. Borg's interminable words trailed away to infinity— echoing, echoing faintly, until he heard no more. . . .

CHAPTER 7:
Warlock, Witch and Guru

A curiously unpublicized fact about Hollywood's Sunset Strip is that it has two distinct sections; the Big Strip, and the Little Strip. It isn't noticeable at first even to the native as he travels from Schwab's at Laurel Canyon, clear through to Doheny and beyond. One takes the mixed worlds of Sunset Boulevard for granted along the general Strip, from the *haut monde* motif of Ciro's, Cyrano's to the leather shops, the special boutiques, the sidewalk cafes, the skin flicks, and the gaudy discotheques. But the very flavor of the better places starts the subtle contrast going. On the one hand, a Parisian-Italian and even Belgian atmosphere haunts the glass and portico charm of the main shops. Here and there between the banks and lawyer-agent facades are such names as Trianon, Charisma, Le Chandail, Columbine, and the Via Condotti. On the other hand, just beyond Palm Drive where the former Writers Guild became the Old World Restaurant, the Little Strip begins. The psychedelic shops and the hip signs *(We Have Super Grass)*, the true bottomless joints *(Nude Amateur Night)*, the homosexual cinema 16s, the hang-outs—all proclaim the longhair Mondo Mosaico of the Anti-Establishment. . . .

The Psycho-Rama was one of those borderline shops on the Little Strip which prospered raggedly, an exotic parasite in the weed ecology of the splintered Mod. Between the extremes of way-out existentialist booths and the strictly hip love-bead parlors, it offered broad ramifications into such related realms as parapsychology, pseudo-psychology, mysticism, witchcraft, and demonology. Behind a garishly purple facade that was once a cigar store, the long, narrow room was intriguingly cluttered with all the tinkling, twirling charms, baubles, and fetishes that the trade would absorb—the atmosphere suitably low-keyed by dim lights, rose incense, and a hint of harp and zither from a hidden hi-fi. Here behind a showcase of psychedelic candles and crystal balls, Mike Havelin incongruously examined the merchandise. In fact, a book on astrology had caught his attention. With Dave Duqayne still missing, this was the last subject that J.A. Hart would have expected him to have on his mind. It was the last place he would have expected to find him. Yet he would have had to admit that it was typical of Mike's modus operandi—always poking into the damnedest back alleys. . . .

It was the chapter on ancient astronomy that had caught his attention . . . something related to Lillian's nightmare. He and her father had become deeply concerned about her after she had sobbed out her wild story about Dave's imagined "visitation." The psychologists were calming her down and she was beginning to admit she had been a trifle masochistic in her self-torture over Dave's disappearance. Apparently she was recovering; yet a few "dark corners" seemed to remain, and Mike's tyrannical curiosity was at it again. In the back of his mind something had stuck concerning her symbolic hallucinations regarding Brockway. Aries and the Ram.

This book was explaining the Vernal Equinox.

"Is there anything here you would like?"

He turned to study a statuesque yet lissome female in a braless low-necked gypsy gown of russet stripes, and scintillating greens, who wore gem-set silver serpentine bracelets and multiple-beaded necklaces. Her lambent eyes were dark gold, her heavy cascade of hair a dark copper hue. On her sensitive full lips was a cryptic smile that could seemingly launch a menacing aura of very special magnetism. It wasn't an act. The young woman was virtually ingenuous in her apparent sincerity, even arresting in her subdued spiritual potential. After all, he reflected, some of these hips did find a curious adjustment, doing their own thing. This one was a lusty flower on a maverick vine.

"Yes," he grunted with a defensive bluntness. "I'm waiting for Larry."

A troubled frown clouded her eyes. An outer shell seemed to clamp down on her briefly revealed mystique. She assumed a sudden hardness. "Look, he *got* the message, mister. He said he'd be out in a few minutes."

Mike checked his wristwatch. "Do me a favor, honey," he said. "Tell him to quit stalling. I want to see him—I haven't got all night."

"Hey! If you're pushing caps—" She bit her lip, obviously realizing by his look that she had made a mistake. "I mean, Larry isn't—" She was getting into deeper water all the time. After all, her boyfriend *did* have a record.

He grinned at her, but with just enough irony to disconcert. "Go tell him, sweetie."

The girl cast him a searching look from under synthetic eyelashes. Reluctantly, she undulated away from him into the rear of the store, trailing jasmine perfume. She was hard to believe. If Larry was the warlock Cyprian, as confided to him by Lillian, then this supple young witch must be Heidi, otherwise known as Melusina, high priestess of the coven. It was impossible to ascribe to either of them the powers that Lil had mentioned, and yet—seen through a glass darkly—who could define the shape of the human psyche? For just a moment there, standing close beside him in the dim magician's shop amidst the candles and charms, she could have been Hecate herself in mortal form. Mike was no mystic; it wasn't his cup of tea. The extrasensory bit always bristled his hackles. Hence he had been gruff, though haunted by her.

About a minute later, Larry came out with the girl doggedly in tow. He was tall, blond, longhaired, heavily mustached and mutton-chopped, lithe and burly under flapping buckskins and beads.

"Look, Havelin!" he warned, petulantly. "I changed my bag, man—I'm staying off! So, like don't make the scene any more—you dig?"

"Sure I dig, Larry, but my bag's been changed, too. Can we rap a little in your office?"

Larry's handsome, hirsute brows swagged mightily together in mercurial suspicion. "Hey now, baby, you aren't the real fuzz, are you?"

"Nope. But I'll level, Larry. I need some help."

"Sorry, man. Fresh out!"

Heidi slid pale soft hands up Larry's heavy arm in a gesture of practiced possession. "You heard him, mister. Now you better split, okay?"

Mike looked around the dingy store speculatively and saw no customers. "All I want from you is a lead, Larry. Is that too much to ask, for a *bill?*"

Larry's soaring belligerence froze in mid-flight. The girl acted startled, then fearful again. "You mean, like, a thou?"

"That's what I said. No strings."

Larry brushed a brawny hand through his tawny locks and glanced at his chick, who watched him warily. He beckoned with his head. Mike followed.

∞

Alberto Moretti was a consumptive old man, but a genius. He worked hurriedly and efficiently at his task, dutifully concentrating on the very advanced electronic knowledge and skill he was now being forced to apply. His dark, thinning hair was shot with gray, his great brown eyes sad in the sentimental manner of Italians, the once passionate lips now pursed in grim reproach—for life, for sorrow, and against his masters.

That's what they were, those heads of *Family,* weren't they? he asked himself as he worked. Beg a favor just once and you've had it. Pay it back, just once, and you're a marked man. After becoming a bad security risk, his twenty years as an aerospace engineer had gone down the drain, so he had needed "favors" more than ever. That's how they trapped the specialists such as he. Doctors, scientists, engineers, technicians and even bankers—all bore the invisible mark of the Mob, once they made their first mistake. Well, he was old, and Fiorenza and the kids could get along without him now with the "favor" money he would get. He hadn't long to live.

He wasn't sure whether or not the work he was doing was legit or criminal; probably the latter since it was for the Syndicate. But somebody in the Mob knew plenty about electronics. He was only installing his own design of an ultra high-frequency wave generator, a plug-in module in a wall panel. What lay behind that panel was carefully guarded. The suggestion of something very much "under cover" was augmented by the design of this whole subterranean layout. Two stories below the mountain, with access through a concrete tunnel from the four-car garage, and walls thick enough for the Maginot Line, it reminded him of specialist work he had done for NATO in Europe below a nuclear blast shield that stretched invisibly for acres under innocent-looking pastures. Here, above his head, the mansion of Lucho (Blue Chip) Castiglia serenely camouflaged the operation. Below ground there was even more luxury and security than upstairs; rich or entals, deep leather divans, green planters to soothe the claustrophobes, even a floor-to-ceiling lighted aquarium. There was some urgent bustling going on. The boys were installing a bar. Obviously, an important meeting was coming up and somebody *really* big was expected.

Even Blue Chip was nervous about the time. He kept watching the generator installation and looking at his watch. "How long are you going to be with that gadget?" he grunted, glowering at him down a black Toscano cheroot.

"Just about ready for a test," Alberto answered.

"We'll do the testing," snapped Blue Chip.

Alberto, still on his knees before the panel, turned stiffly to raise a quizzical brow. "You have some-

111

one with sufficient training and background?"

"Never mind that. What else do you have to do?"

"Just the coax shield connections. For an interference generator—"

"Well snap it up, and then ask for an escort. Don't try to go out alone. You'd never make it." With that, the reptile-blooded proprietor walked off to supervise work in another section, which took him out of view.

The old man wrapped the faded blue shawl more snugly around his neck. Air-conditioning was bad for him. He looked around and discovered that, for the moment, he was alone. Then something miraculous happened. Alberto Moretti fell automatically into a trance. With quick, practiced hands and small fine tools, he opened the forbidden panel, installed a small package from his kit, and had everything back in place within sixty seconds. Alberto did not know he had done this thing. He only knew that his work was accomplished. When a guard sauntered by in shirtsleeves, heavily shoulder-holstered, he signaled to the man that he was ready to go. . . .

∞

Mike's gamut to contact the Syndicate reminded him of the old nursery thriller about the bogeyman. "Now he's on the first step, now he's on the second step—" It cost him a thou to graduate from Larry to the underground pharmacist, who took two thou for a phone call. But even that wouldn't have turned on the nervous old crook had he not been convinced that the *real* middlemen would be impressed. Leaning heavily on the Hart exchequer, Mike was dangling fifty-thousand out in front in order to camouflage the play. So now he was on the "third step," and the situation was getting just a little cute. For one thing, he was being tailed—not by one person, but by two. . . .

This was a sidewalk cafe on the Big Strip, known as the Flip Side, a sort of Hollywood Left Bank for hippies, underground subversives, and health buffs.

In fact the psychedelic menu was touted as representing the first distinctively hip cuisine in existence—mostly vegetarian. Cooked shoots and greens prepared with mushrooms, onions and melted cheese went surprisingly well with the espresso, and at three dollars a copy one had a right to expect it. The regular hips couldn't afford it. They came in for coffee or juices plus their mutual identity, accepting the tourists and weekend warriors as a necessary evil. The colorful proprietor, Jos (Boondocks) Gahagan, had put a price on curiosity and had won. The Flip Side was always crowded. The tourists were never disappointed. On really swinging nights like this one, Boondocks usually permitted impromptu entertainment; guitar solos, rock combos, or an occasional way-out "mood" recital. It cost him nothing, it added color and variety, and it made the Flip Side the "in" place to go.

However, there was one aspect of the place that might be too far "in" for some, and Joe Gahagan himself was that aspect. He disguised it like a pro—Mike had to give him that. There was nothing as hidden as the obvious. It was a trick so old that it worked. Joe wore his sandy hair and beard as full as possible, and a scalloped-brim sombrero served well to shadow his penetrating eyes. Wearing a cut-down blue denim work shirt in bare-chested bolero style, replete with multi-colored prayer beads and tattoos, he looked for all the world like a hip Trader Horn. And that's exactly what he was. The Flip Side was a successful front for the narc trade—as well as "nark"—so this put Joe on a sort of untouchable interface between the Law and the Mob. He traded in two-sided "commodities," and both sides used him as a poor man's Switzerland. He was Mike's "step three."

The pharmacist had called Joe on his private line. Joe knew Mike wanted to see him and that the ante was big. Yet he carried on as though he had never heard of it. Mike watched the six-foot-three proprietor as he moved lithely among his customers, lean-hipped, tanned like a chestnut and as hard as one. Santa Claus smile, big voice, big teeth, big hands and arms. He was a karate man, a health nut, and wouldn't permit smoking anywhere but out on the sidewalk patio area. The healthiest advertisement of all was the most subtle—you didn't tangle with him. You took the happy side of Joe Gahagan, and you never tried his "flip" side.

So Mike bided his time over a "Village" espresso and concentrated on those who had tailed him. The most obvious one was the braless nymph from the Psycho-Rama, Larry's lusty witch queen. She had tried to make her arrival seem casual enough, greeting him as though it were all a coincidence. Although she joined a group of her confreres at an outside table, she kept watching him furtively, especially whenever Boondocks appeared in the vicinity.

The second party on his tail was the one who had begun to make things "cute." A semi-longhair who leaned more toward the Hollywood rather than the hippie style, he wore expensive half-boots, new and store-bought, an open-collar pink shirt, a cream suede sport jacket, and a flamboyant ascot. Mike had seen him at the doorway of a shop on the Little Strip and had felt his repeated surveillance. What gave him away was his office pallor, his late-thirties slouch, and the fact that he knew no one here. Sitting at a single table behind a discarded issue of the *Free Press* was also somewhat sloppy technique. Undoubtedly a disguised minion of the law. Mike could hardly believe that J.A. would have had him tailed. Maybe it was the State Department's work, through Brother Cain. On the other hand, was the opposition alerted to cover Borg's trail? That, at least, would be complimentary if not amusing.

The most incongruous customer, Mike noticed, was an old Italian character with gray-streaked hair, his scrawny neck wrapped tightly in a faded blue shawl. The man looked miserable, yet he listened patiently to a garish guru, who sat on a barrel in a blue spotlight with a mandolin and recited existentialist poetry. He had noticed the old man come in—hurried, furtive, worried, obviously searching for someone. He had sat down in a back corner as though determined to wait for some desperate rendezvous—not with Boondocks, apparently, because he gave him not the slightest sign of recognition.

To a tremulous suggestion of a tune, though strangely effective, the guru intoned his atheistic chant against the Establishment:

> The grass is green, you tell us,
>   over there;
> But Paradise can be a trap
>   that's got you planned.
> I'll take mine where love comes free,
> And you can rap about the Promised Land.
> You take my youth, you
>   crack my spine;
> Your promises are seas
>   incarnadine. . . .

This weirdo, thought Mike in G.I. resentment, should have been at Binh Dinh and Quang Ngai and found out what comes free. He was physically indefinable the way he sat in yoga fashion on the barrel top, with sad, sallow face and enormous horn-rimmed glasses. But maybe that was part of his technique, to de-emphasize physical presence in favor of his hypnotic voice. The kids sitting at his feet were spellbound. The guru words intoned monotonously and the mandolin continued plaintively.

Mike had been a trifle smug about having grabbed this particular table on a crowded night, but he knew now why it wasn't such a prize. Although it was conveniently located beside the entrance into the inner part of the cafe, from which vantage point he could theoretically watch all areas, it was adjacent to the espresso bar used by the mini-skirted help. While customers crowded by on one side of him, waitress

115

fannies and steaming coffee trays threatened him on the other, until at times his view was effectively blocked in all directions.

On one such occasion, "Queen Melusina" from the Phycho-Rama was able to drift into the crowd that jammed up against his table. She leaned close and whispered swiftly to him.

"Mister! Larry didn't send you here to see Boondocks, did he?"

Her pagan-tilted breasts were poignantly visible in that position. She had evidently forgotten the precariousness of her posture but recovered easily, straightening up and tossing her long hair back as he smiled at her.

"Sure are some way-out names around here," he commented.

She was forced by the crowd to move away from him. Obviously, she was frightened about something. When the people-jam cleared, Mike became aware that he was now sharing his table with the ascot-tie boy who had tailed him.

"Do you mind?" asked this one innocently. "The waitress steered me here. I said I wanted to hear the entertainers."

"Look, sonny," Mike told him quietly, "why don't you go type up a nice report, and tell them I cut you off about here, okay?" As the stranger stared dumbfoundedly, he added, "Whoever sent you—tell them to stick it. I'm soloing this one. . . ."

The man's mask of innocence faded. Resignedly, he reached inside his jacket pocket. Mike placed a restraining hand on his arm. "Don't flash the I.D. I don't want to know."

The man looked at him sadly. "Buster, don't stick your neck out any farther than it is."

"I'll put it this way," Mike explained. "You're tailing, but you're not to tangle, right? I play no groundrules, so if you don't get out of my way you're liable to lose a merit badge. Now *melt!*"

The stranger smiled leisurely. "Sorry, chum. You

116

got yourself a baby-sitter. There's too much going on. In fact—"

The ankle hook had been easy under the small table. Now the knee-ram. Mike straightened out suddenly and the stranger went hurtling horizontally between patio tables out onto the sidewalk. People screamed, shouted, got up and milled about. Mike saw Boondock's bearded face swimming toward him above heads. "Ascot" had picked himself up, hesitating. The leg-throw followed by Boondock's arrival had occupied about five seconds. Mike felt a bear-trap grip on his arm. Faces stared.

He shouted angrily. "When I want a queer joint I'll *go* to one!"

Picture worth ten thousand words, Confucius say. Against that, and the staring crowd, the stranger was helpless. He shrugged and walked down the street.

Joe Gahagan used the momentum to complete their contact. "Come in here, I want to talk to you!" he growled. Roughly, for the benefit of onlookers, he guided Mike inside and then added sotto voce: "Meet me in the parking lot in about five minutes." Then he was instantly a grinning host again, all happy-chappy local color, leading newcomers to tables, snapping his fingers for menus and service.

Mike used the opportunity to make sure his tail had given up. The Psycho-Rama priestess was no longer in sight . . . and both the guru and the sick Italian had disappeared. . . .

The parking lot was long and narrow, squeezed against the bluffs which towered up abruptly on this portion of the Strip. Headlights flashed on suddenly. A blue El Dorado lurched to a stop in front of him, driven by Gahagan, who had discarded his sombrero. Mike got into the front seat with him and the car took off smoothly, turning into a winding street that led upward into the hills. There was no conversation, so Mike had a quick moment to reflect on something that his companion may not have spotted. An accidental glimpse of two men in shadow behind the Flip

Side. Just a dim backwash of the El Dorado's head-lights had picked them up for a brief second. One was the old Italian with the blue shawl. The other was the guru. . . .

In about three minutes, Joe Gahagan arrived at a tourist lookout high above Hollywood. The Cadillac lumbered over a low curb onto a precarious parking patch that faced a formidable drop-off. The city slanted away toward the sea like a limp blanket of fallen stars and dying embers.

"Okay, buddy," said Gahagan. "It's still your nickel, so what's on your mind?" He locked brakes, turned off the engine and the headlights. His big beard and shoulders gave a silhouette impression of Al Capp's comic character, Hairless Joe. Only just now at this close range there wasn't anything comical about it.

"Actually, nothing that's real hot," Mike told him casually. "All I want is a certain contact, and I can pay for it. Ten points to you."

"What makes you think I can help?"

"That part's already paid for."

"You're not very smart, buddy. In fact you could stub your toe real bad, making a dumb play like you did."

"What do you mean?"

"You were tailed, goddammit! Tailed to *me!*"

"Maybe we should get one thing straight," Mike suggested. "You're coming on like a big number. The fact is, you're a poor man's nark—"

Boondock's big frame seemed to swell up, turning tensely toward him. Mike knew the man's powerful legs were getting set for sudden action, if need be. "Cool it, Joe," he continued. "Compared to the size of the operation, we're *both* just shit on a stick. Let's cut the dog and flower show."

Gahagan snorted hotly. "Man, you got lip! You know that? You might not get home tonight, talking like that. You're a snotty bastard. I think you're fronting for some heavy muscle or you wouldn't have the guts."

"Put it any way you like. What I want is a *real* contact—somebody high in a local Family, like a *caporegime* or a *consigliere*."

Gahagan grunted, or it might have been a snicker. "Wouldn't everybody! But I don't have to argue. Look—you said fifty, okay. Where's my five?"

"When I talk to the man."

"First, you gotta qualify, Daddy-o—and for that, maybe you should meet somebody else."

He had flicked the parking dimmers twice, as he talked. It was a signal. Another car lumbered heavily over the curb and drew in alongside next to Gahagan. Two men got out, leaving a driver in the car. Hats, topcoats—the bit. Each of them took over a front window of the Cadillac and leaned in. One look at the pug Latin faces and you were through with the introductions. "Now he's on the fourth step," said the nursery rhyme.

"Okay," rasped the nearest Mafioso in a practiced half-whisper, "you got some business? Let's have it."

"I represent a very high-level organization—strictly private," said Mike. "It's legit, but somebody up there made a slight mistake."

"Such as?"

"Embezzlement."

"On the lam?"

"Naturally—but also bad off in the head. There's a bullet in it."

"What from?"

"Attempted suicide. But this executive knows too much that isn't in the files. It would be embarrassing to my clients if he died before they could get that information."

"So? Buy a sawbones to fix him up. What's the angle?"

"The best inside docs haven't got the talent—they say the bullet's in a place that spells curtains if they touch it."

"What's that got to do with us?"

119

"Well, I told you this outfit's high *up* there. High enough to know that *you* boys have a knife who might be able to do the job."

"Oh, yeah? What's this doc's name, if you're so smart?"

"I don't know. We're just making the offer. You rent him to us. We pay. It's as simple as that."

There was an odd silence which seemed to disturb even Boondocks. Finally, the other Mafioso spoke. His tone was more polished but commensurately colder. "Boondocks," he announced, very quietly, "I think your friend is being naughty."

"What gives?" asked the big man nervously. "I thought this was just a clean pass—nothin' hot. . . ."

"He said a no-no. He'll have to take a ride." As Mike faked sudden yellow, the speaker raised a hand gently. "Not what you think, so relax. It's just that when you said this was high level you weren't kidding."

"Hey now, look!" protested Boondocks. "I can't afford—"

"You're clear, baby. We just take him from here, that's all."

"But what the hell did he say?"

"He knows something we didn't count on. He wanted a *consigliere*—that's what he gets."

Boondocks' chin dropped. "You mean—Blue Chip?"

"Shut up!"

"Okay, okay! So take him! I never saw him before!"

Both men leaning in the windows stared speculatively at Mike. The whisperer rasped, "You comin' along on your feet, buddy?"

"Are you kidding?" Mike had his hands half raised in a signal of docility. "I'm a walking lamb!" He was suppressing the heady triumph of a lucky gambler. The setup he had dared to dream of was falling into his lap.

He got out and was expertly frisked. They relieved him of his Police Colt .38. He was secretly thankful he hadn't worn his favorite Smith and Wesson .44 Magnum. Boondocks only sat in the Cadillac and stared at him. Mike's two escorts gently nudged him toward the other vehicle, which was a long black Lincoln towncar.

At this moment, however, the "hero" arrived, and Mike swore aloud. It was "Ascot," the longhair who had tailed him. He must have parked his car down the street and eased into the scene while the proposition was being pitched. Mike's two escorts froze, holding him gently but firmly between them. The driver of the Lincoln slumped down out of sight.

"Well now," said the new arrival, jauntily, "what have we here?" His hands seemed to be clasped behind him as though he were merely out for a meditative stroll.

"Hey, that's the guy who tailed him!" informed Boondocks, ducking low in the Cad.

"You crazy son of a bitch!" Mike yelled.

"A setup!" rasped the whisperer, who started to reach for chest leather—but he froze again. *"Jesus!"*

A very impressive weapon faced him. Ascot had hidden all seven pounds of it until this moment. Mike surmised it had to be a gas-operated automatic rifle; apparently a SWAT version of the AR-15 or a souped-up Army M16 5.56 with a shiny new disc silencer. Mike figured the man for at least FBI with that equipment—more probably CIA. What the hell was going on? And why solo on a caper like this? But he remembered a telephone recording in Hart's office: "This is Presidential level. Only Cain and his committee are cognizant, plus the Secretary and myself, *and of course specially processed members of Justice, the CIA, and a few FBI.*" So he had called him a faggot!

"Now then, gentlemen," said Ascot, approaching slowly, "shall we all make a small contribution? I won't ask you to drop your pants. Just the hardware will do."

"Hey, copper!" wheezed the whisperer. "You got

nothin' on us. If you're after this pigeon you can have him."

"*After* we find out what's going on here," persisted Ascot, still approaching.

Mike started to mutter, "Of all the dumb—" But he was cut off when both his captors shoved him in front of them.

"Okay, Fed," announced the Mafioso spokesman just behind his ear. "You can meat-grind us with that fancy typewriter but it won't get you much."

Ascot hesitated as he studied the two snub-nosed automatics aimed at him just past Mike's ribs. The agent ducked as a shot flamed at him from the Lincoln; then he arched in pain and agonizingly dropped his weapon.

"You *got* him, Mugs!" rasped the whisperer.

But Ascot stopped hamming when he hit the ground. He rolled with his "typewriter" while raking the Lincoln into a mist of flying debris. The thugs tried to fire at him, but Mike used a double arm-clutch on their gun-hands, simultaneously lurching forward and judo-flipping both men directly into the murderous machine fire. They were ripped apart before they hit the ground. In the midst of the clatter and destruction, he knew Ascot was getting under cover behind the Cadillac but that he, himself, was wide open to the driver of the Lincoln, *if* the latter could still be alive in all that torn metal and shattered glass.

"Cover me!" he yelled, and dove for one of the guns on the ground. But he was winged before he got there by another shot from the Lincoln. Instinctively he rolled under the Cad, clutching his left arm. Flesh wound; there'd be bleeding, but no lead in him yet. What troubled him about Ascot's failure to cover him was now explained by a sudden scuffle going on. He rolled on through to the other side and realized that Boondocks had scuttled out on that side and gone around behind, jumping Ascot with his bare hands.

The two fighters were yards from both cars. Ascot

came up from the ground and met the big man's karate with an expert sacrifice throw—but he had to scramble toward Mike as another shot came from the Lincoln.

"I ought to let him have you!" said Mike.

"Dive!" yelled Ascot as two new elements entered the battle. They dove back together under the Cad.

A third car's headlights flooded them from the curb. Boondocks rolled for the special M16 and came up in a duck walk, firing the weapon as he moved toward the Lincoln. The raking fire hit windshield glass but only left star-clusters and bullet pits in the approaching car.

"That son of a bitch is armored!" Mike muttered.

Boondocks made it to the Lincoln and started to open the door. In fact, he even got inside, but that was the end. The armored vehicle, which seemed to be a camouflaged and souped-up Firebird, charged down on the Lincoln like a flying battering ram. On impact, the Firebird stopped, vomiting radiator steam and headlight glass, but the Lincoln sailed ponderously over the bluff, followed by a dwindling sound of tortured metal crashing over rocks and snapping trees —then a muffled explosion.

Mike scrabbled through dirt and picked up on of the fallen automatics, but he stopped cold when he saw who he was aiming at. Out of the ruptured Firebird stepped no less an alien creature than the guru, without his ludicrous horn-rims.

"Ye gods!" he heard Ascot exclaim behind him.

"You can say that again," muttered Mike. "What the hell's going on? Hey—guru!"

"Lay off!" urged Ascot.

The guru serenely ignored them both. He went to the edge of the bluff and observed the flaming wreckage below. As Mike and Ascot joined him, he spoke for the first time. "No homes down there. No brush fire. That wreck will keep. Let's clear out."

"Now just a damn minute!" growled Mike, who still brandished the gun he had acquired.

"Do *exactly* what he says," warned Ascot, who seemed about ready to bow three times to the bearded nut.

"Says who?"

"Come on," said the guru. "We'll have to use the Cadillac. I buckled the frame on mine."

"But listen—!"

Faster than a shell game, Mike's gun was gone and he was on his ear. In all his years of karate instruction he had never seen a move that was as fast or as powerful.

"Don't you know what he is?" said Ascot. "Good God! I thought you were an inside man with Hart! Look—I'm CIA all right? We take orders from these boys!"

"What boys?"

"Christ! You're looking at an "O"-Man!"

He was still in the bedroom and it was still night. Seated in a chair nearby was a bodyguard, mildly absorbed in a copy of *Playboy* magazine. The surface thoughts of the man's mind were naked before him; a cynical appreciation of large breasts, a mental note to read the articles sometime, and an awareness of the Meeting downstairs. The chick on page 55 reminded him of Gloria whom he kept in a room at the Plaza. Later tonight they'd shower together, and—Duqayne rejected a perverted vision.

The man was an underling, but a "contract" type who was as capable of murder as a programmed robot. About thirty-five, one hundred eighty pounds and rugged, he lounged leisurely in the black Naugahyde armchair, confident of his killer capacity. In his shirtsleeves, he wore his shoulder holster openly. It was an advertisement that no games were to be played while he was around.

Duqayne chuckled mentally. His baby-sitter had no knowledge of who or what he was. Deliberately, they had refrained from telling him. It was probably the only means of obtaining a recruit. In the man's mind was implanted a very simple order: Keep him in bed. Under no circumstances permit him to wander about the house. If you have to handle him, keep away from his head. Use that hook of yours on his gut—the solar plexus. Neck and jaw areas okay, but not the head. He's had brain surgery. Most important of all, you shoot him and you're dead. He's worth a billion. . . .

Beyond the bodyguard on a full-length stand was a blue parakeet in a silvered cage. Experimentally, Duqayne probed the small bird's mind. He received a black-and-white surrealist impression of a vast universe consisting of four walls and a ceiling, which was occupied by two shadowy feeder creatures. There was some dim reflection also concerning the imminent event of defecation, plus annoyance with lice. By way of test practice, he gathered a mild mental shot and aimed it at the cage.

The bird dropped dead. It simply fell off its perch to the bottom of the cage and lay still.

Duqayne sweated. What kind of monster had he become? To take life, just like that, on simple whim? He hadn't meant to kill the little innocent fluff. It was ghastly. God forgive me, he thought. But he knew he was right in having turned Lillian from him. He was property now; if not Borg's, then he was a prisoner of his own conscience, or of human society at large, whether they knew it or not. Being neither dead nor alive as a normal man, there was only the single recourse of utilizing his frightening wild talents to best advantage before his captors could destroy him—or worse yet, before they could employ him for their own purposes!

For example, there was this Meeting downstairs. This subject was in the guard's mind, but he had no further knowledge of it other than that Mr. Big was down there. It was a Summit Meeting of the international underworld. Drifting through the man's mind was suspicion and resentment, shadow forms of a nameless fear. Something big was going on, something that might be a threat to the Syndicate itself unless this Mr. Big could come up with the answers. No, the guard had never laid eyes on Mr. Big—few people ever had. And that was another thing he didn't like. Grumble, grumble. . . .

Duqayne realized there was nothing to be gained from probing this one's mediocre mentality any farther. He could see for himself. He relaxed completely for several minutes, willing his consciousness to be unaware of his body. Then, when it seemed that he was merely ethereal, he *was*. He stood beside the bed and looked down at his body, knowing that he

126

was now free in the astral form. Invisible to the guard, he simply moved through the closed door of the bedroom and started his explorations. As he wandered effortlessly through luxurious rooms and hallways he could not help appreciating the alarm that must be felt at those high levels of government where it was *known* that mental, or perhaps astral, probing of top secrets was occurring. On a red alert basis, the intruders either had to be isolated and controlled, or world capitulation would be the inevitable result.

So here was he, an inadvertent new counter-weapon. Borg thought he had him under control. He must make him think so until he was sure he could make a successful move. Garage was in the guard's mind. *Stay out of the garage* had been an implanted order. So he moved outside to the two-storey garage and drifted among its long, shining cars. Perhaps a sub-terranean passage? The man's mind had said "down-stairs." So—underground. Aha! Here was another guard! The swarthy thug sat in one of the cars where he could watch the main door, but of course he was not prepared to detect this kind of intrusion. Duqayne sensed from this one another garbage stream of thought but didn't wait to sort it out. Girls again, and money, and something about Brazil. Who needed it? He moved past the cars to a well-concealed panel, which was locked by a digital-coded mechanism. He dirfted through the panel and found himself in a concrete corridor which ramped steeply downward in the direction of the house.

All right. Now he would look in on Mr. Big. He started to propel his disembodied entity down the passage but was suddenly repelled by an unseen wall of energy. The effect was the same as shock—*astral* shock! Unbelievable though it seemed, he had en-countered the ultimate in alien technology. It was a thought screen, and that included astral projections. Instinctively, he hurried back to his body. . . .

∞

A small red light flashed in front of Borg. Thane saw it. So did Blue Chip. They looked at each other in some surprise.

Borg sighed resignedly. "I'm afraid it's Duqayne," he told them.

"Take care of him," warned Thane, "or I *will!*"

"Yes, sir."

∞

In the bedroom, Duqayne raised up and threw the covers back. Borg would probably have been warned by now, so he would have to vacate the premises immediately.

"Hey! Where you think you're going?" The guard stood up menacingly.

Duqayne ignored him. He found a robe in the closet, also slippers. Putting them on, he hurried to the French doors that led to the patio. He knew the guard was moving toward him. He could read the angry threat in his mind. Duqayne turned to stare at his captor and the man stopped. He felt the power gathering up his spine, from the solar plexus, and down from that nameless canopy "above" his brain—yet he thought of the parakeet. Perhaps now his mental strength was exponentially greater. He didn't want to kill, so how could he differentiate between a lethal bolt and stun?

"Listen, crackpot!" persisted the guard. "I don't know who you are but I know where you're going, and that's back to bed!"

The bolt was ready. Duqayne concentrated on triggering only half of its power. Nothing happened. Instead, the guard grasped his arm roughly and pushed him toward the bed. In a sudden panic, Duqayne struggled physically to get loose, and in the next instant ran into a belly blow that doubled him over. A moment later he landed on the bed.

He gathered every quantum of psychic energy available to him, carefully centered it behind his brows, and shot it at his opponent. This is, he *tried* to release it, but the trigger somehow failed him.

Dr. Borg loomed suddenly beside the guard and smiled down sardonically. "You can't do it any more, Duqayne," he said. "Not unless I tell you to."

"But—the *bird!*"

Borg and the guard turned to observe the dead parakeet.

"For christsakes, what gives with this creep?" protested the guard. "Is he a carni freak or something?"

Borg ignored him, returning to Duqayne. "Not in the program," he said. "Humans only. The oversight is unfortunate, however. That was Castiglia's pet." The doctor frowned. "Too many games, Duqayne. We're going to program you into an idiot if necessary. When we want what you've *really* got, *we'll* turn it on—not you!" As Duqayne glared defiance, he added, "You should be grateful, you know. If Thane knew what you've been up to he'd blank you out completely . . . but, fortunately for you, he's very busy just now."

Thane? Thought screens? The capability of "blanking" him out? Robot programming of the mind? And the bird—dead in its cage. . . . Duqayne failed to orient to it all. He breathed rapidly and he prayed to God for sanity. . . .

∞

Before the three of them could get into Boondock's blue El Dorado, what seemed to be a full goon-squad of armed men began to appear from all directions at once. They talked quietly but the message was clear. It was a case of the party being over; it was time to see the Leadman.

The guru whispered a single command to Mike and Ascot: "Go along with this—it's what we want!" He spoke with all the verve and derring-do of a short-wired booby trap.

That is, the guru's confidence seemed high until they were told to get into the back seat of the Cadillac and two of the goons climbed into the front seat. This part was understandable; they were to be driven to HQ. But what shot the props out and left everybody hanging from the branches was the curvaceous and braless hank of hair who darted from the rear compartment and tried furiously to escape. The hoods caught her and she stared forlornly at Mike. It was the Psycho-Rama Queen, little witch-mother Melusina herself, trying to hang in there but with golden eyes too stary-shiny and her mascara gone to hell along with the hep-cat window dressing.

"I'm sorry!" she lamented, rather throatily. "I didn't know. I only wanted to find out if Larry was still—"

One of the thugs slapped her. Mike looked at her as though she deserved it. The guru seemed troubled for the first time, faced by a snafu element in his strategy.

As the Cadillac moved farther up into the hills, with dimmer-lighted guard cars fore and aft, Mike clutched his wounded arm and wished fervently for his pipe, but under these conditions you didn't fool with such things. Reaching into pockets could make people nervous. The atmosphere was edgy enough without straining it more—as illustrated by the short-barrel shotgun that faced them from the front seat.

So all he could do was sit there and fume. The status quo was strictly FUBAR, with no euphemisms allowed. Here he had started out solo to toss himself into the tiger's den on the gamble that he could escape somehow, once he'd located either Borg or Dave. Smart, no; justified, yes. If he had made it and failed, then going down in flames might at least raise a blip on the Omega sensors somewhere. He hadn't known, of course, that a real live "O"-Man was paralleling his track, or that the CIA was running interference. It made him feel like a gap-tooth rooky who had just caught a football pass with his pants down.

Even that situation wasn't irretrievable, since the

"O"-Man favored the tiger-den tour. Apparently it was his strategy also to drop a bomb or raise some kind of special hell inside the Mafia's *Berchtesgaden;* and if so, both Mike and Ascot could still be useful. But now, here they were scrunched into the back seat with an unpredictable witch from hippyland. One *could* consider her as expendable in the action; in time of war it would mandatory. This whole thing *was* war, actually, but who among them could walk over her corpse and go about his bloody business? It was like trying to aim a rifle with a fly on your nose.

To Mike's deduction department, however, the most interesting part of this whole affair was the sudden change of scope. He had started out at relatively safe low levels of contact, like a sniper in search of a pill-box, but he had stumbled into the main defense line. Either it was a lucky fluke or a squeak in the Destiny Wheel that Dave sometimes mumbled about. Certainly Larry and Boondocks were small-fry, even including the boys in the Lincoln. Neither the CIA nor the "O"-Man would be concerned with that part.

It was that the rendezvous Boondocks had picked *just happened* to be in a sensitive area where the enemy Main Guard was concerned. The "O"-Man was there by plan and design; Mike was there by chance. Since his hint of knowledge about Borg had sent up the signal flags, and since Mike's entry into the tiger's den could upset the "O"-Man's machinery, Ascot had found it necessary to block it. But it had gone sour with Boondocks' side-play, so the "O"-Man himself came into the field—probably with full realization of what would happen. You don't fire off M-15s and toss Lincolns over cliffs with an armored car under the main battlements of the opposition. It makes people nervous. Mike knew now that the "O"-Man had merely included him and Ascot as extra pawns on the chessboard.

The odd queen in the game was this lusty-chested gypsy with the dervish personality; a hip chick with one mask and a haunting succubus with the other.

But thank God, at least she wasn't the hysterical type. She leaned against him but was very quiet.

He tensed suddenly when he remembered the old Italian in the faded blue shawl. The man was troubled, very worried about something; he was uncomfortable, out of his element in the Flip Side atmosphere. What would he be doing in a dark parking lot talking to a top-shelf article like the "O"-Man? Obviously, it was vital information—but what? His itch-worms were at it again. Damn! His pipe would be good about now.

"Where are they taking us?" whispered Heidi.

"Shut up!" warned the man behind the shotgun.

Mike expected her to cringe, but a mysterious change came over her. She drew slowly back against the seat upholstery and began to stare intently into space.

"What's wrong with her?" asked the gunman suspiciously.

"She's in shock," Mike lied, while fighting a rash of gooseflesh. What *was* she doing—conjuring up a whammy?

Ascot and the guru studied the girl in silence. . . .

∞

The nice man with priestly tonsure and the clipped black beard sat on the bed and checked his pulse. He told a pretty young lady in a white uniform to bring him food. There was another man who wore a gun, but this one sat in a chair and ignored him.

Gun? How did he know what that hard chunk of metal was that rested in the man's shoulder holster? Evidently there were things he knew but could not organize in his mind. The redheaded lady bending over him with the food had a starched, low-necked jacket. Mammaries, he thought, while staring curiously at her willing dishabille.

The redhead curled painted lips in a derisive smile. "Eat your supper, baby."

He ate the warm supper because he was hungry, not knowing that the spirit lay beyond hypnosis. In spirit he sought strength. In spirit he felt at bay. He didn't like the lady's smile, and maybe the bearded man wasn't nice at all. Perhaps the younger man with the gun was his enemy!

After supper he lay still and explored himself inwardly. As though held back by an invisible wall, a titanic force swirled restlessly in shadows, demanding release. But something said to him that he was not allowed to release it. He must lie dormant and not attempt to harm anyone. How could he harm anyone? Even his arms and legs were useless. He couldn't move them. He lay there like a brainless idiot. Yet he sensed vaguely that he was some kind of freak who could be dangerous. Moreover, associated with the thought of harming people was a great haunting shadow—a horrible threat of some kind. There had been a name.

Thane!

Immediately the name unleashed a partial vision of something out of delirium or hell. He refrained from shouting aloud in his sudden fright. He knew, somehow, that now he must be secretive. He must be cunning like an animal; he must lick his wounds in silence and gather his strength about him. They had done something to him that held him here helpless for the moment, but they had made one basic mistake. They had motivated him with terror.

The giant force writhing just beyond the scrim of consciousness fascinated him, held out the promise of liberation. Somehow he must find a way of connecting himself with that power. He found that when he closed his eyes and excluded the redhead and her mammaries, and the man with the gun from his mind, then the writhing inner force seemed nearer to him. He learned to think inwardly, more and more deeply.

There was another woman, a soothing blue-eyed brunette, someone who had been very close to him at one time. Her smiling face floated vaguely through his sluggish memory. There had been a book. This dear young woman appeared to be surrounded by books; many strange books concerning the occult, the mind, the human psyche. Often she had read to him, and he could hear her now. . . .

"The human cortex is our chief distinction over the beast. Below it lies the *old* brain, the ancient animal mechanism of instinct. We call this the Subconscious, but it is only so in the gross physical sense. Deeper than this lies the *Un*conscious, the entity of our astral self, which is linked to the eternal cycle of our incarnations. *This* entity is not vulnerable to the technique of hypnosis. . . ."

So that was their game! He had been hypnotized. And now because of this *Thane* monstrosity they had frightened him with, he must find a way of getting around the hypnosis. The half-vision of Thane had filled him with revulsion and hate. Thane was a *thing*, an abomination to the world. He had to be destroyed. Who was there to destroy him? *He*—duqayne, Duqayne, DUQAYNE! His own name came echoing to him out of time and space, and the power imprisoned behind the wall loomed nearer, nearer. . . .

∞

The rambling mansion reflected the inimitable rococo of late Moorish and early Hollywood—a vogue of the gushing Twenties. Yet it projected a certain baleful presence. A brooding malevolence lurked beneath its looming eaves and Spanish arches, moon-mottled between cypress shadows that leaned across its long, grilled windows and terraced gardens. Secluded high in the hills, it looked down on the glittering city and was aloof.

"Y'awl come!" drawled Mike irrepressibly. The cryptic remark surrounded him with blank stares. "Sorry." He slumped, holding his injured arm tightly. His grip on the wound thus far had served to form a massive clot which slowed the bleeding. He did a slight take at the girl, puzzled by her continued trance-like expression.

The somber motorcade pulled in along the entrance drive. Car doors slammed. Figures loomed at the Cadillac's windows. There were words. Something about putting this catch on ice till the meeting was over with. And someone said, "Get something around that guy's arm. Blue don't like blood on the rugs."

"What about the chick? She's got the whammies or something."

"So take her horizontal. She'll feel more at home!"

Matter-of-factly and swiftly, they were deposited in what seemed to be a game room. The windows were small and high up on the paneled walls. There was a single entrance. The door closed, and they were alone with two armed guards, a billiard table, and a luxurious assortment of upholstered chairs, sofas, and other appropriate furniture; including a black leather-topped poker table with insets for cards, chips, drinks, and ashtrays. They were told to sit down, shut up, and wait. The psychedelic gypsy nymph sat back in a deep ox-blood leather chair and continued to stare fixedly at something that lay afar out in Infinity.

In a few minutes a redheaded young nurse came in with first-aid equipment. She knew her business, especially about keeping her mouth shut. She pulled off Mike's shirt and got busy on the arm. Her eyes had a professional way of not missing a thing. She sized up the party swiftly, caught a speculative look from both Ascot and Mike, and put out armor plate a yard wide. There would be no prison "kazatzka" here. No deals. They were cops; they could solve their own problems.

Ascot and Mike were trying to catch the guru's eye, who seemed fascinated by the trance-fixation of the Psycho-Rama kid. So they looked at each other, indicating the nurse. In a way, it spelled things out. The local boys got all shook up when Mike had mentioned a special brain surgeon. Dave Duqayne had been operated on. He had been kidnapped, and the Mafia was somehow involved. Now here was a uniformed nurse on duty—*why?*

"*That's right,*" said Psycho-Rama.

"What was that?" growled one of the guards.

"Not a thing, man," said the guru, glibly. "She's got her eyeballs pinned."

One of the guru's prayer-bead sets ended in an unusual-looking topaz pendant. It seemed to sway hypnotically in the subdued light of the floorlamps. Mike watched it in sudden tense speculation.

The nurse completed the bandage. She picked up her kit and sashayed her kaboodle rather spicily out of the room. A third man appeared at the door and curtly signaled the guards. They followed him out, and the door closed. The sound of a key turning in the lock was intentionally audible.

After a moment or two of silence and a mutual exchange of glances, Mike made a creepy-crawly gesture with his hand along the arm of his chair. The other two men smirked, thus signaling their agreement that the place was probably bugged.

But the smirk left the guru's face first. With a straight poker face, he began to speak volubly in the alley-cruiser twang of an acid-freak. "Man, I don't dig this pad for sour owl shit! I want out, you hear? Like, you cats were rapping about a load of caps . . . so what kind of a bum trip is this? You bastards are fuzz, and on the take at that! You better flip this scene for me and the chick, like *now*, daddy, or I'm gonna wig out!"

While he went on with this jargon, he gravely tapped the topaz pendant. He pointed downward as though toward a basement of the house and made unmistakable signs that something was planted there. After another few gestures, it was clear that the pendant contained a device for suddenly converting the entire estate into a bomb crater.

Ascot covered for him with loud "copper" backtalk. "Aw come off it, Flower Boy! This was a straight nark deal and your sheepherder's ass was safe. This thing just went nutty, that's all. They took us for somebody else."

"Yeah," put in Mike gruffly. "There's a big operation going on. Maybe the Feds are onto it. These

Syndicate guys are touchy as hell. It ain't us they want, and they'll find out soon enough. We got an inside number we can call to take the heat off around here, so relax!"

While the verbal pantomime continued, Mike seemed to die a slow death, partially from mentally kicking himself. Hart was right—so was Cain. He had blown their chances by playing hero. If he'd kept his nose out of this, the "O"-Man might have done his job.

"Are you sure about that?" intoned Heidi in a strangely husky voice.

He ignored her, vaguely assuming that she was questioning his fake comment about an inside number. He was too busy beating himself over the head. The bomb idea would explain the old Italian with the shawl; he had contacted the guru to tell him he'd made the plant. No wonder he was nervous! Damn! Maybe they were all expendable tonight. If there was a big enough collection of the world's heavyweight crooks downstairs, and if Mr. Big, himself, happened to be there—

"Oh that's true enough!" said the gypsy. Now her remark had no connection with the conversation. All three men stared at her. Her voice was weird, almost hollow sounding. She looked into space and stared like a medium. *"But I'm here, too—honest Injun!"*

Mike's spine became a shaft of glacial ice. Melusina the witch. Psycho-Rama—clairvoyant! The girl was a sensitive. She was being used as a psychic channel. So Lillian had *not* imagined her ghostly experience. Dave Duqayne could be dead or alive, but either way, *he was here in this room!*

The vast interior of the condemned building was alternately striated by cavernous darkness and haunting shafts of ghostly light from the moon, which filtered down through holes in the neglected roof. The man watching considered this to be a fit equivalent of some gothic rendezvous for spirits and ghouls, which all the more suited his purpose. And that distant figure of a woman mincing her way among the tie-cables and fallen girders—now blending into shadow because of her somber dress, now showing a glint of the moon on her maidenly dark hair and the pale whiteness of her face, or the stockinged gleam of her shapely foot as it tested the rubbled path. This, too, ludicrously completed the classic formula for necromancy or a conjuring of the supernatural. And yet, why ludicrous? he mused darkly. It was precisely the subject of the hour.

From his vantage point in the wide, abandoned loft, he could watch her approach and take time to meditate on the issues involved, which were fraught with both an irresistible mystery and unpredictable dangers. He stood at the door above the iron ladder, while behind him spread the art and symbolism of his "other" calling. It was the secret meeting place of the coven. To Larry, alias Cyprian, it had all begun with a phone call "out of the blue." Since the unexpected was always an awakening challenge to the initiated, he had listened carefully, his warlock mentality racing into esoteric paths of cause-and-effect extrapolation. The woman's voice had been low, its tone definitely revealing commitment to her decision. The service requested was both questionable and fascinating. The payment offered was beyond rejection. He had agreed instantly, thus circumventing the power-dissipating effects of conscious reasoning, and simultaneously augmenting the psychic potential of instinct. Like a casting of runes, the destiny pattern was now irrevocable—for *her*.

Instinct, the compelling flash of intuition, was Larry's talisman—the very character implanted in his painstakingly carved and exorcised alraun of the rowan wood. He had no rationale behind his warlock status other than that it harmonized powerfully with his vibrations. Heidi, that succulent succubus Melusina, had met those vibrations and augmented his witch fixation. Their hip backgrounds and avant-garde existentialism had strengthened their secret personalities. On the surface they were hips, anti-Establishment drop-outs living in gypsy fashion within the interstices of a splintered society that writhed like some great tangled and polluted Worm of Ourubus in the shadow of tottering Babel. Their mutual knowledge had taken the trip back beyond Babylon into the true antiquities. In the earliest pagan sense they were witches, forsworn against modern civilization and, along with their coven members, in mutual search for the signs of a new age, which was foreseen in their spells. Somewhere close ahead in the witches' "steady-state" Continuum—in that fixed Infinite structure of past, present and future which was One—the shadow of a Promethean presence loomed. It was an era of metamorphosis, of presaged Cosmic happenings, and the initiates who rode the cataclysmic wave of change would arrive at the shore of some new country of revelation.

To the outer world, Cyprian and Melusina were Larry and Heidi, a hippy common-law pair who ran a psychedelic shop and traditionally kept just one step ahead of collectors. In his contempt for the modern Establishment, Larry had been frustrated by the limitations of his poverty. He had often considered profits from the narcotic trade as furnishing an end which justified the means. He'd never pushed the debilitating and crippling hard stuff; just acid, caps and grass.

But to Heidi it was too dangerous. She had made him swear to cut his connection with Boondocks, so when Mike Havelin had offered to buy a contact with the narc crowd, Heidi had flipped. Then he'd gotten this secret phone call and had suddenly disappeared. She must be worried, he thought, but she'd have to sweat it out. What he was going to do now, and what he was going to get *paid* for it, would solve their problems forever.

Or would it? There was something about this Havelin deal that stirred up his clairvoyant juices; it raised a dimly looming cloud of warning. What spiced the mystery was that this gorgeous female climbing the iron ladder toward him was intimately connected with the former detective. Did it all tie into the same kettle? Maybe the time had come to find the answer. He reached down to her upraised hand and pulled her into the attic chamber.

"Have you come prepared?" the woman asked.

"Are you putting me on, baby?" he quipped, from force of habit. "This is Daddy-O number one of the bead set, remember?"

"Larry, please drop the masquerade. It hurts my spell."

"All right, Miss Lillian Hart. So what ritual name have you accepted?"

"The same as when I—"

"When you tried to become one of us before and couldn't make the commitment."

"Yes. I have chosen Ariadne."

"Hmm. . . . Daughter of Minos, the bride of Theseus."

"It is even *more* significant now."

"Why? Numerologically—seven. Let's see, you're Capricorn—that's eight."

"The ruling planet is Saturn."

"Seven—okay. But what about the Bull of Crete? He's Taurus, tied to the Minos legend."

"Labyrinths and a monster figure are in this. Figuratively, I must find Theseus, who is here to free us all from that which destroys. . . ."

"And who does Theseus represent?"

"David Duqayne."

"Duqayne? Hey, wasn't he the partner of Mike Havelin?"

"The same. But let's get on with this, Cyprian!"

The tall, muscular young man with the vigorous blond mane and heavy sideburns seemed incongruous in his rune-monogrammed warlock robe; yet, in the pagan lines of energy radiating from his youthful face and in the glance of psychic power shining in his dark eyes, Lillian perceived the cabalistic authority of the endowed High Magus. His heavy brows lowered at her. "How do you judge the stars?" he asked her.

"The Moon waxes full in my sign," she answered, "and Uranus journeys in Scorpio. . . ."

"The House of that which is secret; death and the occult—"

"Of new life and regeneration," she added.

"Good! You must have known that's why I would agree so quickly. You have chosen a powerful hour."

"Oh Cyprian, I know *more*—your natal configuration, the rare Mutable Cross! Most of it lies within the signs in transit. You're a special wizard and I know your familiar. We must fetch him now—Great Vassago, the spirit of hidden things. He *must* help me find David. . . . !"

"Have you brought your tabard and cingulum?"

She opened her traveling bag and took out the ritual robe, already embroidered in runes with her witch's name. At its waist was the ritualistically knotted cingulum or cord.

"And the mandragora?"

With a trace of hesitancy, perhaps embarrassment, she extracted a carved, smoke-cured figurine and handed it to him. It was the small figure of a man with deliberately detailed genitalia, but in place of the head was a natural cluster of roots supporting a star made of triangles.

Cyprian examined the object critically. "The root?"

"Datura stramonium—from the Sierras. . . ."

"Hmm. The Jimson weed. That fits. You observed the ceremonies?"

She nodded.

"Your athamé? The full deosil in the time of the Moon? The invocations?"

"In Hertha's name!"

"Fine. All the replanting and waiting—?"

"I did it all! The carvings and the words; the water and blood in thirteen parts; the curing in smoke of vervain. We're losing time, Cyprian. It's urgent!"

The high priest gave her an exasperating smile. "You must have intended all along to make the final commitment."

"Ever since Dave started on a path that I knew was deadly, more than six months ago," she answered. "It was an insurance policy in case I had to use it, and now I do. We're losing time, Cyprian!"

"Very well, *Ariadne*. While I set up the altar, you must prepare yourself. . . ."

Lillian felt split into two parts as she prepared herself behind a screen at the back of the loft. The traditions and twisted reference points of normal civilization had left their mark through a lifetime of constant impression; however shallow, they were hard to overcome and ignore. In her "normal" outer self she trembled at the thought of what was going to happen to her now. It was like going across a passenger ramp into a ship that would never return to familiar shores—an irrevocable journey. But her inner self held firm to the thought that if Dave was on a one-way trip, she'd do this to find him and join him. Her greatest justification, which shielded her conscience even from the terrifying final commitment, was that through this strange and darkly gifted Cyprian, she might actually be able to help Dave against the frightening powers that held him captive.

However bizarre her present adventure might appear to the uninformed, she knew that the preparations the warlock was making were practical; they were valid in accordance with ritualistic formulae that had been handed down from a dawn of knowledge preceding so-called "written" history. They were as certain of results as the rising sun. She would be committed, and she would never be the same again. . . .

The wooden floor of the loft had been marked permanently with the full-sized triple circle of the witch's cone, classically known as the Grand Pentacle of Solomon. In its center was Cyprian's low altar table, lighted now by ceremonial candles, the redglowing charcoal braziers wafting ghostly wisps of incense into the still dark air; and the low-flaming thurible of purification with the ready steel athamé and the phallic *baculum* beside it. But what held her eyes first when she entered (ceremonially from the North) were the two figurines on the altar—her mandragora with its carved male genitalia, and Cyprian's personal alraun, a female figurine that boldly displayed the sexual, regenerative attributes of Hertha, mother-goddess of the coven.

A tall shadow emerged from darkness wearing the horned helmet of the grand magister. It was Cyprian, who now waited to know if she was resolved to proceed. For answer, she dropped her robe and stood naked before the circle. He walked toward her and with the ritualized cloth he blindfolded her. There was a moment of waiting in which she knew he had gone back to the altar to pick up the knife—the athamé for the starting ceremony. She fought back tears and prayed to her dead mother to forgive her—it was for love. Then she bit her lip hard and fled to her inner karmic view of reality. These things of the ancient wizards and magi served to wrench the mundane mentality from its rut of norms. They would cleanse and set her free. Only then could she tap the power pool of the coven.

What followed seemed to her lost in time. It was interminable, it was instantaneous; past, present and future bound into a single, soul-tempering experience that was tantamount to reincarnation. Scorpio, the eighth house of secrets, of death and regeneration. The chant of Hertha, the cold touch of the knife-tip to her naked breast, and the priest-guide's challenge: *"Whence comest thou?"*

"From the North, the place of darkness."

"Whither goest thou?"

"I travel east in search of light. . . ."

It went on and on . . . the ligature, the sprinkling of salt, the earth pentacle between her lips, her presentation to the cardinal compass points in succession, her symbolic purification by the basic elements of earth, water, fire and air. . . .

"Listen to the words of the Great Mother who was called of old among men Artemis, Astarte, Aphrodite, Dione. . . ."

∞

Dr. Jules Borg, alias Herman Mael and certain other names, was worried because he was worried. He had always been too clever not to have the odds covered at every turn. Was he not playing the most dangerous game in the universe? Even against Thane? Therefore, to find himself in this vague state of apprehension *was* cause for worry. He knew the source; it was his human guinea pig. He did not choose to think of Duqayne as a Frankenstein creation. Rather, he was like a nuclear experiment in which a chain reaction might result unless he kept it under constant control. To create a superweapon against Hell itself, one would have to play with the fire of the gods, and this was what he was doing.

The metaphor he liked best was Pandora's box, especially the Greek meaning of Pandora: *all*-gifted. Duqayne's new brain was the box, the dangerous gift that could contain all evil and the power to destroy. In a far-off place and long ago, he had learned the maximum taboo of anatomical science: *synaptic totality.* In Duqayne he had turned it on; the patient could become like a critical mass, his mental power could increase exponentially; in the end, a madman or a

144

messiah could rule the universe. The trick was to cork such a forbidden genie into a bottle for one's own purposes.

Naturally, he couldn't have achieved the long dreamt-of operation without help and organization, so he had sold his plan to both sides. The underworld was suspicious of a mystery figure like Thane, a man who demonstrated such an awesome charisma of dictatorial leadership. The grand *capo di tutti capi*, master of the total world of crime. So, on the side, he'd convinced such leaders as Castiglia and his peers that Duqayne could become an insurance policy against unexpected heavy-handedness by Thane, and/or his unseen associates, if any. And Borg alone knew there were Overlords above him.

Of course Thane could see all this in their minds, and so Borg allowed Thane to read his own intention: to insure *Thane's* side against an insurrection in the ranks. Most important of all, to utilize Duqayne as a super-genius for solving the riddle of X, once it was in their hands. Knowing the way-out method that Thane would employ for its theft, Borg knew that X would soon be theirs, so the Meeting in progress was aimed at plans for its exploitation.

As to the matter of diverting Thane's prodigious mentality from his own secret thoughts, Borg was especially proud of how he had achieved it. A unique mental development of his own devising, which he called "multiplex consciousness."

So it was that Borg was troubled over the fact that he was troubled. As he sat in the all-important meeting with Thane and Castiglia, while the plan was being worked out with thirteen world leaders in crime and spurious finance, he had an instinct that Duqayne might counteract the deep hypnosis. He deliberately telepathed the thought to Thane, so the latter hardly took notice of his departure. Thane mentally agreed. Their Promethean child had to be watched. With him he took the wrist-transmitter that controlled the "screen." In an emergency he could drop the screen and telepath to Thane from a distance. He gathered an impression of Thanian satisfaction as he left, but a wave of suspicion was picked up from Blue Chip. Borg knew he would be followed. He was prepared for it.

So far, he felt triumphant. Once he was far enough up the passageway to be beyond the thought screen and safe from the all-knowing Thane, he relaxed his mental control and let his secret thought run naked like an imp. The theoretical reason for the screen was twofold: to forestall any possible probings by Omega, in case they had progressed this far in the paranormal sciences; and to keep Duqayne from eavesdropping. But the *real* need for the screen was a double-sided secret. He knew that Thane wasn't so much worried about Omega probings as he was from possible penetrations by powers that lay even above his own status in the dark pantheon of his breed; since they all read each other's minds and tended to become one monotonous baleful entity, perhaps it was a longed-for relief to the Overlord to relax in an oasis of private thought. Or did Thane also have secret plans of his own? As for Borg, his own real need for the screen now was to keep Thane from sensing how dangerous Duqayne was becoming. If the monstrous entity knew that Duqayne might one day pose a threat to him and his kind, he'd burn him out as he had burned Kettleridge—instantly, and without compunction. *Naturally* without compunction! The thought of Thane having a twinge of conscience was so incongruous that the worthy doctor was forced to smile—but only momentarily.

So engrossed was he in his own machinations that he had failed to sense the approach of Castiglia behind him. Blue Chip overtook him in the garage. They both nodded to the guard and then hurried toward the house together.

"If it's hot enough to make you bug out from the meeting," said Blue Chip, "then it's something I better take a look at."

"Actually," countered Borg casually, "my mission is purely medical."

"You mean that sexy red head can't look after your guinea pig?"

"Not quite. He's still critical. However, now that you're here, maybe you can put our new guests on the grill. Find out what they know."

"Yeah, dammit. They may be Feds. But the guy to grill is that think-tank of yours. Why's he that important to them? *They* don't know what you turned him into. He's been six months out, terminal, kaput! Why the big action?"

"My friend, the opposition only pretends to have dropped the Kettleridge case. Duqayne is no doubt regarded as a key to it—and to *us!*"

"Well, we got him now and they can go suck air. If your caper with Duqayne works, they won't have a chance, anyway."

"That's what I want to make sure of."

"Okay. You go check on your Band-Aid Houdini. I'll take a look at the gate crashers. As for the meeting downstairs, it's all decided. We know what to do. Thane's just hearing himself talk now. These big-time turn-coats are all the same. . . ."

As Borg went his separate way toward the bedroom, he wondered in grim amusement what this top *consigliere* of crime, this bloody-handed sadist and contractor of organized murder, would do if he knew that Thane was infinitely and terrifyingly more deadly than the mere traitorous double-agent and one-man brain trust that he was pretending to be. . . .

∞

The *old* brain, the "ancient animal mechanism of instinct"—this was the barrier that locked him from conscious control. That part of him lay in hypnosis, closing a door against outward locomotion. But traveling *inwardly* was unrestricted. He could enter a deep inner darkness, a world without barriers of time or distance; a place where unseen mind called to unseen mind in unspoken whispers where mental affinities were fields of force, somehow, arcing in seeking, probing, tentacled traceries of bluish light, like bridges of Being across infinite chasms of psychic Limbo. Among the trembling and wavering traceries lay a powerful shaft of deeper blue that drew his urgently, and he sensed a name: *Cyprian!*

Suddenly he was using another person's eyes; a female person whose mind or psyche was powerfully receptive to him, even binding him to her as though by a spell or entrancement. They were passengers in an automobile, and a man faced them from the front seat with a shotgun.

"What's wrong with her?" asked this one.

"She's in shock," answered a man beside the girl.

Duqayne was aware of pain, and of bleeding. The man next to him had been wounded. There was an affinity bridge between him and this man; an old friend, perhaps—

But the girl who had locked her inner mind with his was making other bridges. Across the chasms of the inner world, both he and she seemed to travel as though of one mind—to a place that she sought desperately, to a place that he now realized he must also discover. And then both of them were looking through another double pair of eyes, a scene he could not at first comprehend. . . . The vision was not clear or intelligibly oriented because of an apparent dimensionlessness in terms of time and proportion. Nirvanalike, he had a sensation of being every*where* and every*one* at once, there in a cabalistically appointed loft in some vast, abandoned building in the dead of night beneath a waxing moon.

Instantly he was caught up in a vortex of new and powerful energies. He was aware of rising intensities of psychic lights in the inner worlds—bright tendrils of violet and blue with chromata of red and orange— strangely exciting colors and forms that seemed locked symbolically in a wild-whipping dance of pagan power. Minds were locked here in a concerted crisis call, and he and his female catalyst seemed to coalesce mightily into a common cone of force.

There was the altar table with a crystal sphere enshrined on a wormwood block within a ritualistic triangle and braced by candles in an aura of frankincense, saffron, and balm of Gilead. The two who knelt here wore pentagram amulets of protection and were locked in trance concentration upon the crystal, *seeing* it limned with a bluish flame of psychic energy. He heard and understood their invocation, to which now his female guide added her impressive power: "By Satander and Asentacer, by Beldachiensis and Liachide, we conjure thee who knowest the secrets of Elanel. . . ."

As it went on, his vision was timeless, his awareness quadruple; there was a Cosmic remoteness yet an intimacy deeper than self. He knew this woman as his own flesh, this raven-haired witch at the altar, and he knew the intensity of her desperate emotion which had brought her to this commitment—saw again the naked ritual, the talismanic blessings by the warlock magister, understood the mental cleansings and the pagan euphoria of new birth, felt the rising field of force to which he now inadvertently added an unmeasured power. He was quickly alerted to the emergence of some massive presence; there was a sense of beast smell and ancient wisdom linked with imperious warning. In the crystal ball, a haze of gray mist, then the coruscating symbol of Vassago. . . .

"Lo! I am here. Why do you disturb my repose?" The vast thought-voice was all-encompassing, abysmal.

Simultaneously the alarm struck all participants, giving them sudden total awareness of each other. Duqayne felt the horror of Cyprian at having interference while in the conjured presence of the demon. He tried to withdraw from a rising colossal shadow, but in a lightning transition, those bound in the force cone were hurled through time and space to the mansion on the hill.

"A trap, Cyprian—for Vassago?"

"No!" cried the warlock priest, in obvious confusion. "No, Vassago! I did not know!"

"Forces are here which endanger me. Thus cast yourself into the crucible and be damned!"

"Wait!" Duqayne's own thought intervened. "You are right. There is danger here. But free me, and I will join in the counterattack!"

He sensed the demon's swift departure, then Cyprian's flash of intuition. "Who is here?" asked the mental voice of the warlock.

"It's Duqayne!" interrupted Lillian's mentality. "David we've found you!"

"I am bound," said Duqayne.

"Then we shall release thee," said the warlock, eagerly. A flavor of revelation and ambition laced his thought.

"Cyprian!" cried the girl who had guided Duqayne. "The license of release for Vassago—make it or he will destroy!"

"Go and release him, Melusina—quickly! I have work here."

Lillian's entity joined her priest in the task of dissolving the hypnosis. Duqayne caught their psychic vision of will; saw the chains on his subconsciousness smitten by lightnings, and he was free.

But in that moment the abyss of the inner world was rent by a scream of anguish.

"Melusina!" came Cyprian's thought. "She doesn't have a protective pentacle!"

Seemingly without effort, Duqayne transferred them to the coven loft and blocked the psychic death-grip of the demon spirit. There was a moment in which a wall of titanic energy rose against him; a sulphurous wave of blasting heat writhing there but withheld, poised like the head of some cosmic cobra, ready to strike and sear his soul with fangs of hateful destruction. Yet he sensed intellectual curiosity on an Olympian plane.

"Who leans thus his mind against me?" came the infernal thought. *"Art thus of the Brazen Vessel—lost these many ages? A Lord of the Djinn?"*

"I am new born," Duqayne found himself saying.

It was an answer coined of instinct but strangely appropriate. "Spare the witch, for I would use her. A friend. . . ."

Cyprian incanted rapidly. "Vassago, we license thee depart into thy proper place, and be there peace between us evermore!"

"So mote it be!" said Lillian.

The demon force swept back into the far oblivion from which it had arisen. The girl, Melusina, now fled with Duqayne to their separate physical locations, while in the moon-striated loft the warlock and the witch awoke to the trembling relief of being alive.

"You fool!" growled the warlock. "What *is* this Duqayne of yours? You didn't tell me he was superhuman!"

"I didn't know!" wailed the witch. "Oh God, I didn't know!"

"But, in that other place, where we freed him—Vassago was aware of danger to *himself*. Was that danger Duqayne, or something even greater?"

"Something *else*—I'm sure of it!"

"Then God help us all!"

∞

When Blue Chip entered the game room, three guards joined him, guns out and ready for action. Ascot, Mike, and the "O"-Man were gathered around the gypsy girl asking questions. She still sat in the ox-blood chair and stared in trance, speaking rapidly in strange hollow tones.

"Whatever the plan, strike now," she was saying. *"I am free. . . ."*

"What the hell's going on here?" snarled Blue Chip. "Hey—cover those kooks!" he commanded of his men. "No games. Hit 'em if they move!"

Castiglia's thugs moved forward, ready for a kill.

∞

Borg entered the bedroom just as Duqayne rose up

and swung his feet to the floor. The gunman moved to deter him again, but Borg waved him off. "You don't *really* think you're going anywhere, do you?" he asked.

"Yes," said Duqayne. "Your party is over, Borg. I'm leaving."

The gunman and the redheaded nurse in the starched, bosomy smock stared at Borg, who again signaled them to cool it. "He may be delirious. Let's see what he does. I assure you, he's harmless. . . ."

Duqayne put on robe and slippers and glared loftily at the doctor. "Sorry, Borg. I said it's over with. You'll just have to get the hell out of my way!"

It wasn't what he said that caused Borg to blanch in alarm; it was the psychic atmosphere surrounding his patient. Sheer menace and power now; no trace of hypnotic control. He nodded suddenly to the gunman, who rushed Duqayne eagerly.

The man stopped in mid-charge and dropped to the floor, unconscious. The nurse also slumped into a curvaceous panty-stockinged heap. Borg felt a shock-wave of numbing power—it was a stun, which he resisted. But it took every erg of psychic energy he could muster. "Duqayne, you fool!" he shouted. "Without my guidance you'll be destroyed!"

The next wave was no stun. The doctor sweated, struggling against a searing bolt of force that bent his consciousness slowly downward, until he fainted. . . .

∞

"O"-Man turned to Castiglia's armed thugs and raised his hands in mock hysteria. To the Mafiosos he was only a longhair guru freak, so the act was convincing enough.

"Okay, man," he whimpered, "cool it, will you? You want my ass, you take it. But like, don't make with the lead! I just came along for the ride!"

"All right, the rest of you!" barked Blue Chip. "Let's have it! You're Feds or alley fuzz, which is it? Spill now or fold. There's no time to dick around!"

"Please!" wailed the guru, throwing himself at the feet of one of the gunmen. "Don't crack my spine! I'll sing, I'll crawl, but lay it off me, will you?"

"Shut your yap!" growled the thug. But he screamed then in pain as he was karate-groined and his gun flew.

The show was on, with Mike and Ascot dodging artillery and flipping flesh. Furniture crashed, kneed faces spurt blood and teeth. The "O"-Man was a vicious blur of vengeance. One man lay dead, his rib cage ripped by expert fingers. Another choked on a ruptured trachea.

Castiglia whipped out his gun and covered them all. He shouted an icy warning. They paused, a tattered cameo in mayhem, staring into a tensely-gripped .45 automatic.

"I'll blow the shit out of any man who moves!" he gutturaled. His glacial eyes were deadlier than the physical threat itself. Like scar tissue ready to blight with a curse of hell.

The gypsy girl's eyes finally focused on reality. She collected her succubus limbs and rose up slowly to her dainty feet. Her stare toward the door swiveled all heads, except for Blue Chip. But he was alerted to a menacing presence behind him.

Duqayne seemed priestly in his turban of bandages, tall and gaunt in his lavender robe. He moved into the room with monstrous certainty and began to instruct. "All right, everybody," he said quietly. "You will proceed at once with your plan."

Blue Chip whirled and tried to pull the trigger but was frozen where he stood. He stared like a horror face in stop-frame, incapacitated by a mental vise he couldn't comprehend. Mike Havelin chopped his wrist and the gun clattered to the floor.

"O"-Man!" commanded Duqayne. "Your pendant!"

The guru grasped the necklace pendant at his throat. He flipped it open gingerly. "Now?" he queried, mystified.

"*Now*," said Duqayne.

The "O"-Man pressed a button. There was no physical explosion as had been expected by Mike and Ascot. The Italian's "package" behind the secret panel downstairs emitted an ultra high-frequency wave that stunned all hands on the hill, thus demonstrating the fact that Omega *was* in the race concerning the paranormal sciences. In the meeting room below, all members slumped into mental stupor, and that figure which represented Thane did the same. However, from its fleshly cage emerged an entity that was mutated beyond Man before *homo sapiens* walked the Earth.

In the game room the effect was the same. All slumped to the floor except Duqayne who staggered under the impact of the psychic blast but did not fall. Castiglia, supercharged by a will of hate that was inhumanly bestial, managed one final act, rolling to the gun and firing it as he went out.

The bullet struck true, lodging dangerously close to Duqayne's super-adrenalated heart. . . .

∞

Down the hill on the snaking concrete road, a string of armor-plated cars with dimmers balefully glimmering. Inside, at least five of the new NATO M-15s and an authority to match. A red light blinked on a special panel; the "O"-Man had triggered the Psi-Bomb. J.A. Hart looked at his watch. When he glared questioningly at the Security Council staffman and the State Department rep, they nodded.

The ominous caravan flashed a rash of headlights, sprouted red-swirling roof lights, broke out with a scream of sirens. All cars dug out, converging like mournful banshees on the secluded mansion above them. . . .

∞

Duqayne stumbled through downhill underbrush, a crimson hand pressed against his chest. In bitter self-appraisal, he stubbornly avoided contact. Let Omega take the hill, he reasoned. He had personal questions of his own to answer—if he lived.

There was a terror that pursued him. He had sensed its presence, far more colossal than that of the demon Vassago; he had been convinced that his signal to the "O"-Man would unleash the force that would destroy him. But at least he could be the decoy; he could fill the inner world with a mental star-shell, drawing the dreaded Nephilim evil toward himself to spare the others. It was there. It came upon him bat-winged in lethal intent, yet too loftily egotistical to measure his strength. A stench-laden darkness iced his soul; a pyschic wave smote him to earth, sending his brain reeling through molten sheets of pain. Then it was gone like a giant's heel in passing. He lay there gasping for life, bleeding into a mat of weeds and twigs. Somewhere a cricket strummed its mating call; a plaintive chirp in the infinite void of ghastly revelation. This was the day of the Demon, but not yet the night thereof.

"Duqayne!" came a distant mental call. It was Borg, struggling titanically to recover. *"Your strength is too precocious. Out of control it will destroy you!"*

"I believe the word you used, Doctor—was exponential. Thanks to you, and certain of my familiars—a very swift recovery."

"Touché for now, Duqayne! But you have only made yourself a target for the final test. There will be 'other' visitations. Do you understand?"

"No doubt there will be, Dr. Borg. I don't doubt it at all."

Borg alone had resisted the Psi-bomb impact sufficiently to be on his feet in time to act. His mental
search convinced him that Duqayne evidently had
elected to play the rogue bear and withdraw into personal hiding. For the moment, it was a matter of
salvaging the remnants of the *Alpha Plan*. The bodies
in the bedroom and down in the game room he found
to be merely unconscious. Obviously, Omega was moving in. It was all devishly clever. Now he knew that
his repeated warnings to Thane had been justified.
Omega technologies and techniques were developing
faster than anticipated; the time for definitive action
was unquestionably close. Duqayne had to be found,
and stopped, before he could join forces with them.
Thane had retreated somewhere in his customary lofty
manner; no mental contact in spite of the screen being
down.

His first rallying point was Castiglia. There might
be no time to rescue the Syndicate leaders from downstairs, but at least he could salvage the top *consigliere*
—then backtrack for contact with the elusive Thane.

So it was that when Omega arrived at the mansion, three important persons were conspicuous by
their absence: David Duqayne, Dr. Jules Borg, and
one Lucho (Blue Chip) Castiglia. As for the coveted
Mr. Big, the shocker of the evening was the rigid
figure in the center chair of the conference table—a
shriveled, mummified corpse whose grinning death's
head stared in hollow-eyed mockery at a council of
peacefully sleeping Mafiosos.

On the normal government levels of FBI, CIA, and
the Justice Department this was the biggest criminal
haul in years, a virtual triumph over the international
underworld. Notes and recordings on hand could cinch

a speedy mass-indictment on charges of maximum conspiracy aimed at the national security. The case was more solid than if the miscreants had been caught redhanded with an atom bomb.

But for Omega, as such, it was a frightening crisis. At the Lodge, at the Ranch, and across the Atlantic at MI-7, the alarm panels strobed orange flashes in a peculiar sequence—a message from the computer entity known as the "Bug." This was Omega Alert, Condition *Two*. The evil miracle of the death figure in the council chair had more than clinched the ultimate inferences of the Kettleridge affair. The so-called Aquarian Age was darkly shadowed by something hideous, unknown, and cosmic in magnitude. As J.A. had put it so aptly, the "lid" was off. . . .

∞

"John," said the President, "before you fire up the panels I want an appraisal. How long do we hold Condition Two—and how many of the scenario points support it?"

"*All* points support it," J.A.'s chin cleft was prominent—no finger-tapping now. He was grimly decisive. "As for how long—until the points drop or increase."

"*Mister* Hart!" interrupted the Pentagon representative. "*We* are here to determine—"

"The Commander-in-Chief will determine," Hart snapped instantly. "After we come up with something to determine *with!*"

"But—"

"We also have a twelve percent level for a Condition *One*." Hart had already dismissed the interrogator. He was activating the consoles, again bringing in the Lodge, Washington, and MI-7. On the black-lighted world map, a small amber blip traced the course of a plane somewhere over Michigan. Senator Cain was en route to the West Coast again. He was being tied into the conference while in flight.

"He's right, Colonel," conceded the President.

"Sir," the Pentagon emissary persisted, "with all

due respect, we should clarify our positions. My job here is to determine facts and reports to the Joint Chiefs. Now there are certain questions—"

"Time we don't have," Hart interrupted, struggling to control his temper. "Your questions will be answered, or probably disqualified, if we can get started."

The bird colonel fumed, still not surrendering, but the President shot him a signal to cool it.

"As you say," Hart added through his teeth, "we should clarify our positions. Omega is *not* running the government, but this isn't one of your contract procurement hassles. Nobody's in here sweating to cop a hunk of tax money for his own side. We're figuratively in a bomb shelter with one thing on our minds: *survival*—not as a nation but as a species. Now hopefully that ought to drop your hatchet—and young man, I suggest you keep your eyes and ears open for a while, and maybe pray."

The President raised a brow at his Secretary of State. Wearily, he nodded to Hart. "All right, John, link us in to the Bug. Let's have it all."

They sat at their assigned monitor panels—at least the main four consisting of the President, the Secretary of State, J.A. Hart, and one of Mike's newest companions in arms, a deceptively quiet young athlete named Ron Stanger. Now in a slim jumper suit and with a G.I. haircut, he could not have been recognized as that same guru of the Flip Side who had turned magically into an "O"-Man. Those without available panels sat in viewing seats directly behind the main four. These men included Mike and his other new buddy, the CIA man he had nicknamed Ascot—alias Jerry Macklin—plus of course the squelched bird colonel. As for the normal coterie of presidential bodyguards, the ultra-high level of secrecy had required that they remain outside. It was unprecedented, but so was the situation.

Mike watched it all with his usual bulldog tenacity. It was his first Black-Button confab since his "O" man indoctrination. The presence of the Chief Executive underlined the gravity of an Omega Two—a super hotline situation. Since the raid on the mansion he'd been burning for action to find Dave, yet he knew he couldn't solo this one. The picture was too big. He wondered how in hell anybody could come up with anything more logical than running amuck. All too incredible, too udefined, too way-out to lend itself to any existing formula of counter-strategy. However, these were the Brains and the Authority, he reasoned. He was prepared to listen—at least for the moment.

Brockway was curiously absent, temporarily out of contact, but Hart had waved it off as one of his academic quirks. On the other hand, this factor may have triggered Cain's decision to come out personally. Something was going on that Hart and the senator were not articulating even at *this* level of security, and Mike was determined to track it. Was J.A. running scared? He'd soon find out. . . .

There was a rapid phase of briefing review aided by the Bug. Some final orientation here—an answering of questions. The Bug was a very flexible and semi-portable computer. It was practically a walking CPU that could be plugged into various operational modes, at the Ranch, the Lodge, or elsewhere.

"He's a growing boy," commented Hart, "and he's learning fast—also linked up to data banks across the country."

"We used him to hypnotize the Italian," added "O"-man Stanger.

"You mean brainwash," corrected one of the Security Committee on monitor 2.

"Whatever. If they'd read Moretti's mind they wouldn't have known he was going to plant the Psi-bomb because he didn't know it himself."

As an "O"-man initiate, Mike's biggest jolt had been the unveiling of *X*. At first he hadn't quite understood all the clock-and-dagger about it. Certainly it had the same breakthrough status of the A-bomb at its inception, but considered in that light alone he could only give it a normal top-drawer classification. However, when the full ramifications were explained to him he finally understood why it was the biggest thing since the wheel—or fire. It was an all-time bonanza but also the Gordian knot—simultaneously a golden key to the human dream and a sacred white elephant big enough to squash the world. X had been dubbed "The Box," which was short for Pandora's box—a cosmic goodie bag containing gifts of the gods that came with a pricetag maybe too big to pay for on the human level. But the Box existed. Human civilization would never be the same again. No constitutional form of government was geared to administer it, because by its nature it demanded an international superstructure for even considering its maximum applications. In the wrong hands it could give absolute power. So the concept for Omega had been born, even embraced with relief by the two nations that knew about it.

As Hart pointed out, the satus quo had no precedent whatsoever outside of biblical references. When one's new model of the universe said that nothing was supernatural anymore, that the old superstitions had been replaced by a concept of "higher energy levels" which were now regarded as parallel universes or extra-dimensional realities—then one tended to double-bolt the gates. *Anything* could come through; and because of *X*, there were monstrous shapes at the door. It was relatively a time of miracles but not of angels. Death stalked the Earth in demonic form. Only the God-given mystery of cussed human perversity, or the raw animal instinct of survival, could guide them now.

"Or maybe the Bug," said Mike at this juncture. "We're pretty damned emotional. At least that thing can sort out the significant pieces."

Meanwhile the Presidential party had taken off for other emergency conferences elsewhere, towing the bird colonel with it. But the Secretary had remained, along with the tense faces on the monitors. Everybody agreed with Mike's suggestion, including Cain, whose plane was still moving steadily westward on the map. They sorted out the pieces and Stanger fed them into the comforting computer presence. It was Pyrrhus at Delphi begging a divination.

There were details of the raid on the mansion that made the whole thing more personal for Mike. He was called upon to reexamine his own observations about it. Ascot and Stanger supported him here and added some of their own.

"There's no doubt about a blood trail," Mike concluded. "And Castiglia's gun had been fired. That was just forty-eight hours ago. As far as I'm concerned, Dave is either dead by now or in need of a friend. Is there any way you can get that damned Bug to boil down a clue? I *thought* I was pretty sharp once along these lines, but now when it counts, my skull is solid bone!"

Hart knew that it was always difficult for Mike to show his inner feelings. "You're too close to it, Mike," he said.

One of the Lodge council members moved in on another phase. "John," he asked over the monitor, "are we deliberately avoiding the subject of Duqayne's apparent ESP?"

This was good for a lively round robin, both on the screens and in the Tank. When Dave had appeared in the game room he had demonstrated a strange new transformation. There was also Lillian's wild tale about an astral visitation, also the Psycho-Rama girl's story—the demonstration of her clairvoyance. As for the witchcraft episode reported by Lillian, by Heidi, and by her warlock boyfriend, this was still too much for everybody present—apparently. . . .

"This thing isn't normal," said Mike finally. "So maybe that's our trouble. We've been trying to *think* normal. It may be we're driving against the traffic."

"Could be," Ascot agreed.

"All right!" snapped Hart. "If this is game theory, let's play games. No holds barred. Even if you think you're nuts, come out with the craziest idea that hits you—*anybody!* Don't mull it over first. Just *say* it!"

Finally it was Stanger who broke the impasse. He pointed out that the Bug's programming was heavily gated with NOR-logic based on human reasoning constants. He suggested that they remove some of the human factors and let the computer draw conclusions directly from the data—*all* data, no matter how improbable.

A recess was called while Stanger and Hart worked with the Ranch programmers upstairs. When everybody went back into the Tank there was a desperate air of expectancy, also an unspoken feeling of personal relief. If somebody had to be crazy, then let it be the Bug. There was a human limitation to going against ingrained reason. Their minds were tired. They were grateful for a crutch.

"So the Bug is on its own at this point," added Stanger. "We've asked for an unrestricted summary."

"Is it ready?" asked the Secretary of State.

The Bug itself replied. The readout board came alive with a race of lighted block letters:

PROJECT GENESIS: SUMMARY
UNRESTRICTED WITH TERM HQX ON
   COUNTER-INVERSION

GIVEN:
1. PSI-PHENOMENA ESPIONAGE AS
   RECORDED
2. FACTOR 1 SUPERIORITY OF AGGRES-
   SION AND/OR RELATED EVENTS AS
   RECORDED
3. INCREASING FREQUENCY OF ITEM 2 AS
   RECORDED

CONCLUSION:
HUMAN CIVILIZATION CONFRONTED BY
POINT-NINE-SIX PERCENTILE PROBA-
BILITY OF SUBJUGATION OR REPLACE-
MENT BY SUPERIOR INTELLIGENCE OR
SPECIES

Before anybody could react to this, the board wiped clear and an afterthought was added:

DEFINITION SUPERIOR ORGANIZATION
NOT QUALIFIED IN THIS SUMMARY
RE HUMAN PHILOSOPHIC CONCEPTS OF
GOOD OR EVIL

"Wait!" warned Stanger as a hubbub started. "He's still reevaluating the data banks."

The readout board darkened, then suddenly spelled out another addendum:

CORRECTION:
PERCENTILE PROBABILITY SUBJUGATION
OR REPLACEMENT HUMAN CIVILIZATION
REDUCED TO POINT-FIVE-ZERO

"Hey!" yelled Ascot. "That's a breakthrough!"

Hart also jumped. "A fifty percent *chance?* Where did *that* come from?"

"Precisely!" said Cain over the speaker. "Stanger, ask it where that sudden factor change came in?"

Nobody in the Tank was sitting down. On the monitors, even the phlegmatic MI-7 chief had risen to his feet. Hart hovered anxiously over Stanger as he programmed the computer: *Trace logic basis for percentile change at output DGA.*

Within thirty seconds the Bug replied:

PRIORITY OF *X* NOW SUPERSEDED
X IS NEUTRAL FACTOR
NEW FACTOR DYNAMIC WITH NON-
LINEAR ELEVATION

The board cleared. Another four words raced acros it:

IF CAN BE VERIFIED

"That Bug has gone crazy!" exclaimed one of the Council members at the Lodge.

"Wait! Hold it!" Hart demanded. "Dynamic factor . . . non-linear rise. . . ."

"Exponential," said Stanger.

"Well, dammit—*ask* it! What's the new factor? For Christ's sake I can't imagine *anything* more earth-shaking than X!"

"You mean," said Cain, "*if* its potential is developed. The Bug is intimating we have something on the front burner we've overlooked."

"I think I know what it is," said Mike. All faces stared at him. He shrugged. "Don't take it from *me*. Ask the Bug."

Stanger keyed the question in through the language-converting programmer board. *Define new factor changing percentile at output DGA.*

The board glimmered fitfully for a moment, as though a child's mind were groping for new expression. Then a name appeared:

DAVID DUQAYNE

An uproar ensued. The Lodge Council and the Security Committe rejected the logic basis; i.e., Mike's unrestricted idea. Most of the Bug's logic would rest on the witchcraft testimony in that mode. But Hart, the secretary and Senator Cain managed to focus the issue to some degree.

"What the Bug is trying to tell us," Hart summarized, "is that Dr. Borg converted Dave into some sort of super-wired mental mutation, whereby he's not only able to tune in on the Opposition's wavelength, but also able to give them a run for their money with their own kind of ordnance. This of course would iron out the credibility of the witchcraft story, the girl Heidi's clairvoyant demonstration, Steve's ability to speak through her, and ultimately to escape."

"It would also mean," added the MI-7 chief, "that Mr. Duqayne is your long-awaited super-weapon. . . ."

"Keeping in mind," cautioned Stanger, "that the Bug has qualified this. He said: *'If*-can-be-verified'. . . ."

"Meaning," said Hart, "that Dave's got to be found first."

Mike cut in swiftly. "Gentlemen, if it's true, and if the *Opposition* knows it, Lillian Hart will be the target."

"What!?" Hart paled, staring at him.

"He's right, J.A." It was Cain again. "Your bulldog is still in there. They'll be scanning your daughter *mentally*, watching for any telepathic contact from Duqayne. But I think the girl can be helpful to us for that very reason."

"What do you mean, Charlie. As a *decoy?*"

"Something like that."

Mike frowned angrily. "That's *her* decision to make!"

The filtered voice of the senator came back through the speaker, aggravatingly unruffled. "Perhaps, Mr. Havelin. But remember, *you* brought it up."

"Charlie, now just a minute!" interjected Hart. "You want to break up the ante in this damn game, then show your hand! The *real* reason you're coming out here personally. If you don't break the silence, I will!"

All faces on all monitors stared questioningly at Hart, who locked a father-son gaze on Mike accusingly. In the Tank, the remaining men looked expectantly at the flight-link speaker.

Cain replied, "All right, John. I *was* holding that ace up my sleeve. It was to win a point with the President. There is one item of latest news that your Bug doesn't have. If he did, you'd probably be at an *eighty* percent level for a Condition One."

The Secretary of State intervened. "Senator, you know the rotation. I represent the President here. I'm requesting your information."

"All right, Mr. Secretary," said Cain. "The information is this: All thirteen of the Syndicate members who were being held in Los Angeles for remanding into Federal custody, have disappeared."

"What—from the County *jail?*"

"That's right, from the maximum security section, too. But worse than that. It wasn't even mental control over the prison guards. Video monitoring canceled that probability. The prisoners simply disappeared—poof!"

"But—*how*, for the love of God! That's impossible!"

"Synonymous with *miracle*, I'm afraid. We have here a positive demonstration of mass teleportation. Factor 1 amplified."

"Jesus!" whispered Ascot.

"Now on the strength of that, Mr. Secretary," continued Cain quietly, "I have a new plan to propose, and I'll expect you to obtain Presidential support for the strategy—probably to override the objections of Mr. Hart, himself. I believe it's the *only* answer to getting some forward momentum worked up on Project Genesis."

Hart fumed at his old college buddy. The Secretary of State listened to Cain's amazing plan, and Mike froze.

"I won't have it!" exclaimed Hart. He turned to monitor 1, appealing to his colleagues at the Lodge. "You're the Omega Council. Dammit, where's your support!?"

The Council member who appeared to be the spokesman answered him. "We know how you feel, J.A. But what if your daughter agrees?"

"That isn't the approach I'm suggesting," interrupted Cain. "I'm requesting a Presidential order to *draft* her."

Mike couldn't help it. He shouted. "*Up yours*, Senator!"

There was another moment of *very* respectful silence. Then the speaker rattled. "Don't blow it, Havelin. You'd better quit while you're ahead—all right? This happens to be war, and the Goddamnedest war you ever saw—I use the terminology deliberately. I

166

believe it was *you* who suggested that human logic has two left feet. We're trying to avert an Omega Zero. If we can override the *emotional* factor out there, we may have a chance. As for the personal side —John, Mike—my plan is the *only* approach to locating David Duqayne. And Mike, you challenged us to think *ab*normally. We're doing that. As for psychic dangers to Miss Hart, she's a self-confessed witch. What higher qualification could we ask for?"

"Okay, Senator," retorted Mike, "and you, too, John —and your whole council up there at the Lodge. Speaking of breaking the silence, why not make a clean sweep? In all of this you've been doing a rain dance around an open question."

"What is that, Mr. Havelin?" queried the secretary sharply.

"Brockway! Your top boy on the K-chromosome research, and the one who dug up Dr. Borg out of the blue. Right in the middle of all hell breaking loose, Dr. Irving Brockway shows up missing!"

Cain cut in happily. "Precisely *again,* Mr. Havelin! So happy to have your support! That was a most interesting report you filed concerning 'dark corners.' Miss Hart's *own* suspicions regarding Brockway were most enlightening. She *couldn't* be more qualified for this mission."

Hart fumed darkly at Mike. The Tank was silent. There was no sound except for a distant hum of generators.

CHAPTER 11:
The Great Unknown

The meeting in the Hart mansion was unexpectedly brief, as tough words had run out. A status of action remained.

"It won't require a Presidential order," announced Lillian, quietly. "I'm a volunteer."

Cain had not arrived yet; he had gone first to the West Coast White House to guarantee his position. Hart and Mike were present in the living room along with an Assistant Secretary of State, plus "O"-Man Stanger and a well-oriented Lieutenant General representing the Joint Chiefs.

"Don't look at me that way," she told her father. "If you and Mike can hand over your personal sovereignty to Project Genesis and Omega, then I at least offer *myself* if it will help to find David. . . ."

Hart shook his head fretfully and stared at the Box on the coffee table in front of him. "I always kept trying to tell myself I could keep you out of this, Lillian, but I guess I knew all along—"

"Don't blame yourself, Mr. Hart," said the Lieutenant General. "Blame the enemy. It's as simple as that."

Hart touched the Box with ill-concealed wonder. It was black plastic, six inches by six, and eighteen inches long, completly sealed. "That's right," he answered. "The bigger things are, the simpler—such as the awesome simplicity of natural selection. You take this Box. It's sitting here like a package of meat from the corner market. But all of the world's tomorrows could emanate from it. If it's grabbed by the enemy, mankind could possibly terminate its career on this planet as the ruling species." He lifted his gaze, searching every face around him slowly. "Sometimes I wonder if we *are* sane. As Mike says—two left feet—at a time we can't afford it."

Mike got up. He had to move, pace the floor. "You're right. We're nuts! There's no way out of it. It's a commitment. Irrevocable. But I don't have to like it!"

Ron Stanger reached into his pocket and extracted a string of colorful beads. "It's time to give you this," he said, handing the necklace to Lillian.

Mike watched her as she hung the string carefully about her neck. It harmonized somehow with her plain black dress. Her dark hair was down around her shoulders. Wearing no makeup, her pale white face seemed translucent with some new but somber candle of awakening. Since her witch commitment, she had shown a change of personality. It bugged him now that he could only see her as though through a scrim; a veil between two worlds. Cain was right, blast him! She was a perfect candidate for the final strategy. "You sure you know how to use the amulet?" he asked her.

She fingered the same topaz pendant that the "O"-Man had used at the mansion. "Oh yes, Mike." She smiled wanly. "The Bug has me programmed."

They all knew that the Bug had processed everybody present. Various planned areas of suppressed memory or conditionings to be triggered on cue made a complex of semi-reality where no one could be certain of just who would now react to what, or when. It was a safety measure against alien mental probings.

The plan, as far as they understood it consciously, was reviewed. A mental probe of Lillian would reveal that the Box was now in her keeping. This made her the world's Number One Decoy. But the pendant had been revised; it offered two types of signals. One, of course, would trigger the maximum-powered Psi-bomb that had been installed in the house—enough psi-level energy to put the neighborhood to sleep. This other signal tied to Omega, to Hart's office, and other strategic points. If Duqayne contacted her in *any form*, she was to transmit the signal instantly.

It was a part of her programming.

"Don't forget what I'll be doing in the meantime," she reminded them.

"I'd *like* to forget it!" said Hart, and Mike seconded the motion.

"After all," she smiled without humor, "there has to be *some* method to my madness. Besides, I think Cyprian's plan is valid."

Mike couldn't take any more. She was changed from the woman he knew, but she was hung out on a master bull's-eye for the biggest nemesis in history. His only contact with sanity was the grim promise of some unfinished detective work. "Come on, J.A.," he said. "I've got some chores. I'll drop you at the plant."

"Mike?" Lillian got up suddenly and came to grasp his hands in both of hers. Her blue eyes searched his face. For the first time that evening, the old Lillian came through the veil. "Don't lose me." He stared at her fixedly. "I mean, you've got to grant me my own salvation. To stay even half sane, to stay alive at all, the adjustment *had* to have some warpage. Do you understand?" There was a faint glimmer of tears. "I've *got* to find Dave!"

"I understand," he said, wanting to take her into his arms but mentally kicking himself again.

He went out to the cars with Hart, followed by the general and the assistant secretary. There was a presentiment of walking into the night of life, itself, with a reasonable doubt about any more dawns that would be the same again. In the house with Lillian was Stanger, plus two other special guards. The "O"-Man was a strong point there, Mike knew. The other two were comparative window dressing. It was a simple setup, but how simple could you get?

As for that crazy setup in the basement, Hart had no way out but to make the concession to his daughter. In fact, some of the Lodge Council and the crowd at MI-7 had considered the experiment with some respect. After all, they argued, this was part of the *psi* of it all.

When Mike and Hart drove back to the plant, they couldn't know consciously what the Bug had suppressed in them; that was on vault-locked mag tapes at the Ranch. Yet they assumed that there was more behind Lillian than met the eye. And they were right. In a one-mile area surrounding the mansion was enough compact Federal and Omega fire power to obliterate all fifty acres of the estate in a single flash—but the parameter that could trigger such an event was known, at present, to the Bug alone. Or so it seemed. . . .

∞

When a man attempts suicide by refusing to breathe, the involuntary factors take over and force his lungs to keep working. In a mutant there can be higher ramifications of the same principle.

Duqayne had a reason for choosing death, but his bleeding had been too much of an alarm for his system. A combination of new locomotor, neurological, and endocrinologic controls plus a subliminal autonomic guardian that was superhuman had served to stop the hemorrhaging before he realized it. But the *bullet* was there. With a clairvoyant eye, he could see it pressing dangerously against the main vena cava and the aorta. Continued exertion could restrict the main artery above his heart, and it could all end soon. There were shooting pains. With an awareness of his own masochism, he was glad. Death would be welcome relief, a final escape from the overwhelming and incomprehensible thing that he had become.

As he had moved down the hill, marveling at the instinctive perversity of his body in its blind attempt to survive, he had reviewed the dilemma morbidly. To preserve Lillian and all who were close to him, he had to get out of their lives since his very existence now made them targets. On the other hand, should he choose to turn the tide against Borg and his alien allies, and should the effort result in the slightest degree of success, then his forced role as a messianic protector would be ordained forever. Where would be life itself? Moreover, his existence could only heighten the degree of danger for the world at large. He was a causal *part* of the current emergence of all the dark miracles. A Lord of the Djinn? Hell no! He was new born, but an unwanted irritation in the cosmic plan. The only conclusion was death.

Now as he lay in the darkness of the one remaining sanctuary he could find, he was quiet, taking advantage of reason to double-check his conclusion. Ever since the witch and the warlock had freed him from the hypnosis, he had become aware of the astounding scope of his capacities. The mental perspective, the brightness and swiftness of amazingly complex thinking processes, the clarity of his inner vision—an armory of wild talents he hadn't yet measured. He could reach out into the streets and see through another's eyes, read and control minds for blocks all around. The taxi driver who had brought him here would not recall he had picked him up. There was even telekinesis. As he lay there he made tassels dance on Lillian's reading lamp. No one knew that in the lonely beach cabin a monster languished in angry discontentment, dangerously keyed to the potential for violence or self-destruction. There was even teleportation. That hateful ebony voodoo mask with its crown of brass. He narrowed an eye and it was gone, suddenly to appear in the sea tides beyond the shore outside, sinking down to oblivion. But Lillian's hand-made parchment caption remained on the wall. He brooded at its runic mystery, aware of the stabbing pain next to his heart, which came now with almost every breath.

There was a temptation to contact Lillian just once more before he died. But no. He was a contamination to her. It was better to die, and with him, hopefully, would die the whole damnation of the Kettleridge affair. In the inner mind, the psychic darkness pulsed and flickered with delicate traceries of feeble light; human mentalities groping unconsciously outward from a million petty dreams. They were *safe* dreams. He retreated, hiding his nova light from that deep abyss where unknown lightnings waited, probably watching for him to emerge.

They would watch forever, but in vain. . . .

∞

When Mike returned to the penthouse headquarters of Hart International, the hour was late. J.A. was winding up some Omega details on the project. He was in the company of his bright young assistant, who saw in Mike's urgent expression that his swift departure was desired. The battered briar was fuming fitfully.

As the aide left the suite, Hart picked up a sheaf of classified documents and squinted curiously at Mike. "That burner of yours is sending up smoke signals in binary," he commented. "What's the translation?"

"I'd feel better if you went home, J.A."

"I'm going, but take it easy, Mike. Lil's protected. In fact I got a call from Stanger about half an hour ago. Cain's on his way."

"He's staying there?"

"It seems a good strategy. I may have some recent sore points with him, but he's moral support, nevertheless. We can see this through together."

"How will he get through the security? The Bug must have provided—"

"That's programmed in. Cain can get through. So can Brockway."

"*Brockway!*"

Hart stared. Mike raved. "Jesus Christ, are you *insane?* You know Cain's suspicions about him—"

"Mike, that's enough. here are some things you don't know. I sent Brock on a private mission."

"I don't give a damn *what* you sent him on! If he gets into that house you might was well throw in the towel—it's over!"

"Goddammit, Mike, you'd better put your money

where you mouth is! Now let's not waste any more time. Spill it! What the hell's grinding you?"

"Okay." Mike sat down. So did Hart. He was unsettled by the high rash of anger and turmoil on the other's rugged face. "John, I told you about Lillian's suspicions, her premonition about Brock's mental surveillance of her that night. . . ."

"Oh hell, we've been through that. Come on!"

"Just cool it, John. I'm going to let you have it. Now listen. As far as that astrology reference is concerned—"

"What? Aries and the Ram?"

"You betcha! The Vernal Equinox, my friend. Brock's ego caught him off guard. His parables are showing. He dodged her birth-date question, but he said he was born 'long before sunrise.' And he *added:* 'The sheep were asleep in the meadow.'"

"All right. I'll be impressed. Go on."

"That's the clue! The sheep, the Ram. Aries—the Equinox. To be born when Aries was not yet in the Ascendant would have to be *thousands of years ago!* Irv Brockway is a goddam Nephilim, a K-chromosome head man. Otherwise known as Mister *Big!* A nice house guest you're expecting, John. You blew it!"

J.A. swelled visibly. He jumped up and yelled a dirty word. "Mike, you've let me down, you crazy ass! I don't buy it! For God's sake, you take a piece of hypothetical guesswork like that and expect to throw it against the entire logic frame of the Project Genesis scenario? Dammit, you're acting like a punk flatfoot with a screaming case of the Ouija boards!"

The phone rang. Hart grabbed it off the table. "Hello!" he practically shouted. Then he went slightly rigid, staring across the receiver at Mike. "Yes, fine. All right. I'll be there shortly, and help yourself to the bar. Stanger will—"

"Who's that—Cain?" asked Mike.

Hart paled, gripping the phone hard. "They did *what?* Good God! Are you sure? Where's Lillian? Okay, okay—we're on our way!"

Mike waited. Hart ran for his coat. "Stanger and the two guards have disappeared into thin air—it's starting to happen!"

"John! Who was that on the phone?"

"It was Brock—but thank God he's arrived!"

"What about Lil?"

"She's up in her room. Come on—let's move!"

Mike took hold of Hart bodily and virtually threw him onto the divan.

"You crazy son of a bitch!" Hart yelled at him.

"*Listen to me,* dammit! What I told you was just for openers!" Mike took a folded newspaper from his coatpocket and threw it at him. "Look at that paper! It's the L.A. *Times,* Night Final, June 15. That was the night Brock was here in your office. I got that copy from the *Times* morgue."

"So what!"

"So *look* at it! Do you see any front-page spread about Borg?"

Hart stared incredulously at the paper.

"We were *scammed,* buddy. Mental control! *Now* maybe you know where you caught a whiff of sulphur from, eh?"

"Jesus!"

"So *who's* a flatfoot?"

"Mike—if he's the *one,* why would he phone me?"

"Who knows *his* brain? Perfectionist? Hostages, maybe? I could be wrong, J.A.—but Mother of God, I don't think I am!"

Hart got up hurriedly. The two of them moved fast to the gold-tinted glass doors—a portal into the Great Unknown. . . .

∞

Lillian emerged from the elevator in full witch regalia; the long dark hair almost at her waist, the protective amulets, the runic robe and knotted cingulum, the red velvet ceremonial garter. On her mind was the thought that she just had time to get back to the basement before the cone of force was closed.

But suddenly a nightmarish *presence* seemed to alert her instinct. The dimly lighted hallway developed those same "dark corners" which she had sensed before in Brockway's presence. She tensed, her fingers automatically seeking the "O"-Man's special amulet. Her heart began to race.

"Is someone here?" she asked, then turned, startled, to find her father standing behind her.

"I didn't mean to scare you, Lillian," said John Anthony Hart.

For a split second, she hesitated, but then finally she threw herself into his arms with apparent relief. "Oh Dad! Dad! I tried to get you at the office. I've been on the edge of going into a flip!"

"It's all right, Lillian. You can relax now. We've heard from Dave."

She stared at him, fighting a wave of shock. "David! Where?"

Hart smiled gently. "Plans are changed, and you'd better change that outfit. I'll get the Box. We're going to him."

"Oh God!" She should have been crying, but her eyes and her lips were suddenly parched.

"Hurry now. We can't delay."

Lillian ran to her bedroom and entered it without another word. In the hallway, Hart smiled in quite another manner. He headed for his own bedroom, intent upon retrieving the Box from the safe.

Perhaps he was too exhultant to back-track on what was going on behind him. After he had left the hall, Lillian reappeared from her bedroom, her pale countenance drawn into taut lines of near panic, which struggled there with a deadly resolve to hold onto her sanity.

If this apparition were Thane—Brockway, or whoever—this masquerade in her father's form would figure—the ultimate sophistry of the Demon. Had the Bug programmed her sufficiently to block her thoughts from him? The amulet was in her hand, yet the expected impulse to fire the Psi-bomb did not arrive. No *positive* proof yet, but a horrifying presentiment nevertheless. She ran into the elevator. From down below she could get on the phone and warn the "O"-Man. Then *maybe*—if God willed— she'd have just time enough to finish the rites that had been begun, to contact David.

The lift door closed. Lillian descended swiftly. . . .

∞

Duqayne awoke from a fitful sleep, aware of stabbing pains. His inner eye could see the bullet, which now pressed heavily in against the straining wall of the aorta. With a little exertion now, he could die. The massive hemorrhage would be too swift even for *his* autonomic guardians.

A last look around. Still the temptation to reach out to Lillian, to say good-bye. The cussed little witch had made a vital commitment—to her, perhaps her soul—in order to find him. The least he could do—

Suddenly, as though it were a message from her, he focused his gaze on the parchment; her runic sign beneath the ebony mask that he had angrily teleported into the sea. The cryptic letters drew him as through with a magic force. . . .

ᘓ ᘐ ᘗ ᘊ ᘉ ᘁ
ᘊ ᘗ ᘜ ᘈ ᘓ

A new, final impulse of irresistible curiosity impelled him. Painfully, carefully, he made his way to her bookcase, fighting against knives of pain. This time it wasn't to get the Holy Bible. He found what he wanted, an ancient book, tall and black: "Conjuration According to the Grimorium Verum." A part of her library of black magic and demonism. He had chided her before, but now? He couldn't know. An impulse drove him to search the pages in a feverish desperation.

The runic alphabet was there. He memorized it

177

instantly. He knew then without looking back at the parchment what it said.

"Oh my God!"

But wasn't his brief contact with the demon Vassago sufficient proof to override the last shred of materialistic doubt? The awesome myth of antiquity —was *real!* Interpret it as one might, whether one thought in terms of symbolisms, mythologies, parables, actual infernos, Nephilim cursed of God, or a K-chromosome race of Earth-stranded mutant beings from the stars—the indisputable conclusion of their existence in fact remained.

He fell to his knees in a paroxysm of pain from the bullet. The aorta wall bulged warningly under the alien pressure. Nevertheless, a stillness fell upon him. He entered the inner mind with a desperate resolve; one final probe into the infinite dark to find her, to see if—

Across the psychic abyss leapt a bolt of blue force. The affinity for *him* was irresistible.

"David, if you hear us—!" The mental cry was Lillian's.

The impact of her terror smote him. It was enough. He pulled out of the trance and stared at the carpet beneath his trembling knees. His clairvoyant eye on the bullet. Another few labored heartbeats and the aorta would burst, spilling his life.

He firmed his will, gathered his concentration. A sudden thrusting of mind—there! Before him on the carpet was the blood-gleaming bullet, the object of some very practical teleportation.

Later, while doing what he must do, while moving where the new impetus of his will to survive now moved him, he stared mentally aghast at his persistent vision of Lillian's runes on the wall. They spelled out a demonic name: SERGATHANUS. . . .

The book had included the name in a chapter entitled, "The Descending Hierarchy." Here was the ancient pantheon of the supposed Inferno itself, starting with Lucifer the Emperor. "Sergathanus" was listed as a high-ranking officer under Grand Duke Astaroth. Laughable, of course, to the layman; but not to Duqayne who had encountered Vassago, an entity also listed there but under the subcaption: "Spirits of the Brazen Vessel, or Lesser Lords of the Djinn."

It would have been ludicrous also to any scientist who was not aware of the Omega model of the universe, which Duqayne had perceived in the "O'-Man's mind. *Nothing* supernatural—multi-leveled planes of energy, parallel universes, extra-dimensional realities. Through the ages men had reduced the ancient truths to superstition or parabolic faith.

What the ultimate explanation might be was not of the moment. Even now he might have fought instinctively against the "impossible" conclusion that Hell was *some* kind of physical reality, but two more coincidences he had encountered became too much entirely for any further defensive rationale. Borg's other name, used in Europe, was Herman Mael, a thin disguise for the lesser demonic name, *Hermael*. And as for Sergathanus—how about *Sergius Thane*. . . .

When Mike and Hart approached the mansion,
J.A.'s car was roadblocked by an armored weapons
carrier. This was part of the Bug's security. Regardless of their obvious identity they offered no objections to the "dip tank" operation, which was Mike's
definition of the screening process. Everything was
deadly impersonal. An armed and helmeted MP placed
Hart's hands on the portable scanner, which was
linked through microwave to the Bug at the Ranch.

"The password, please."

*"And it repented the Lord that he had made Man
on the Earth, and it grieved Him."*

The spoken scripture had to be a long enough phrase
so that the voice analyzer could get a representative
audio sample. A green light flashed as distant micro-
registers responded.

"Clear, sir. Next please. . . ."

Mike went through the same ritual including the
electronic fingerprint scanning.

"That was a tight squeeze," said Hart as he drove
onward. "If we'd told the MPs what we've found out,
God knows what the Bug might have turned on—
maybe a total wipeout from the rocket batteries. . . ."

"I thought the Bug would have those phone lines
tapped. Brock's call—"

"We don't know how the deck's stacked. Our memory of classified data has been suppressed."

"So it's just us chickens."

"Plus Lillian's friends in the basement."

"Same as tits on a boar."

Hart brought the car to a slow-glide stop before
the pillared entrance, his headlights already turned
off. "Christ, if only—" He tensed, looking at the
house. "Who's that?"

"I don't believe it!" Mike muttered. The tall robed figure silhouetted in the open doorway would have been unmistakable even without the bandaged head.

"*I sensed your arrival.*"

"Did you say something, Mike?"

"God! He's telepathing to us! It's Dave—come on!"

Both men got out of the car and met David Duqayne on the veranda.

"Dave!" exclaimed Hart. "All I can say is thank God—there isn't time to say more!"

"Yes there is, dammit!" persisted Mike. "How did you get through that security line, you louse? Where've you been? And what about that bullet?"

"Later," Dave told them. "There's danger inside."

"Where's Lillian?" asked Hart.

"I've lost her."

"Lost her!" yelled Mike. "What the hell!"

"That *thing* has thrown up a screen. I could try to force through, but there's a better way. . . ."

"You're damn right there is!" Mike extracted his .44 Magnum and dashed into the house.

"Mike, wait!" Hart started in but Duqayne detained him. "He's an ass. John, whatever you do—stay behind me. . . ."

∞

When Mike entered the house he was too intent on the staircase and the upstairs balustrade to cover his back, which almost instantly felt the cold pressure of a gun muzzle.

"Sorry, Havelin. This is to keep you out of trouble. Drop your gun."

Mike had felt guns in his spine before. The shock of hearing Brockway's barrel-chested voice in his ear suddenly slammed years of special training into a blur of elbow and a karate follow-up. The result of which was the incongruity of a very large microbiologist lying spread-eagled on the floor.

"All right, bogeyman." Mike aimed the hefty Magnum point-blank at the doctor's nose. "Let's see you pull a voodoo spell on *this!*"

"But I—"

"Shut up! Where's Lillian?"

Duqayne appeared, followed wonderingly by Hart. Brockway's dark eyes widened in an intensity of alarm. "Dave! John!" he grunted as he scrambled up onto all fours. "For God's sake, can you two talk some sense into this maniac? I was only trying to—"

Mike grabbed Brock's gun and prodded him to his feet. "Here's your head goon of the goblin set, baby. He's not so tough now!"

Dave raised his gaze to the staircase. "Mike, you put your dime on the wrong number. . . ."

Mike whirled to a position behind Brockway and followed everyone's startled gaze to the imposing figure on the stairs.

"Cain!" shouted Hart.

The senator stood on the upper flight of the hall stairs, immaculate, dignified, sternly critical of the situation. Under his arm he carried the Box.

"John!" Brockway's low voice carried a note of fear for the first time since anyone had known him. "I warn you—that is *not* the senator!"

Cain began to descend the staircase. "This is the screwiest reception committee I've ever seen. Brock, what the hell have you been drinking?"

J.A. frowned angrily at his old college sidekick. "Charlie, how did you open my safe? What are you doing with the Box?"

Dave spoke a quiet warning. "All of you—get out while you can."

"I tried to warn Havelin," grumbled Brockway.

Hart held his ground, his face hard-drawn but reddened by perplexity. "Dave, for Christ's sake, spell it out, will you?"

Duqayne held his gaze fixed on the figure that descended toward him. Only he was aware of the dreaded ringing in his ears. "I've seen you before, Thane, without your screen. You've come a long way but this is where you stop."

The senator shook his head with a touch of gentle sadness. "Finally cracked, eh? We had hopes for you, Duqayne."

"Hey, will *somebody* fill me in?" complained Mike. He moved into position to cover the senator and Brockway simultaneously with both his guns.

"Yes, please do, somebody," agreed the senator, who finally paused near the bottom of the staircase. "I'm fairly confused, myself."

"Wait!" J.A. placed a restraining hand on Mike's arm. "If this—*person*—is an imposter, where is the real Cain?" He glanced at Brockway intensely. "Irving, do you mean—?"

"That's right," boomed Brock with a confirming nod. "That little trip to the morgue paid off—a little extra work on the autopsy. I'm afraid that the Bug has the most recent picture of the late senator."

Mike stared at him aghast. "Do you mean Laughing Boy—that *corpse* we saw?" Seeing the confirmation in Brock's beady black eyes, he slowly raised both guns, fascinated by a nameless revulsion, knowing that he was going to lead-blast this apparition clear off the stairs.

But it never came to that. In the next instant, Mike stared incredulously at his tingling empty hands. The guns were gone.

"Good Lord!" whispered Hart.

"Teleportation—psychokinesis," commented Brock. "Same as he did with Stanger and his boys. It's also the way he got the Box."

"Dave?" Hart pleaded. "In the name of Heaven, is this really happening?"

"Not in the name of Heaven, John. In the name of Hell or a new-universe model facsimile. He's trying to probe me now—warning me not to try him."

"Then don't!" said Brockway quickly. "I knew all along what all of you were getting into—too much, too soon. But Dave, you wouldn't let go of it. Back off *now* if you want to live!"

The ersatz senator's decorum altered. He frowned

183

darkly. His voice deepened with an alien quality. "Miserable chattering apes! Savage infants in time, opposing life that was old with knowledge before you emerged from the primeval slime!"

"You're *too* old now," answered Duqayne. "Your kind is dying. You conceived of forced mutations like me, new brain-children to help you solve your final riddle. Well, your wish is fulfilled. I'm here at last, the long-forbidden miracle—your dream of ages!" Dave's voice turned flat and cold. "For you it may be a nightmare. *Sergathanus!*"

An invisible "wind" knocked Mike and Hart to the floor. Brockway staggered back against the wall. The false Cain had received Duqayne's leathal bolt head on. It forced him to drop the Box and hold onto the railing with both hands.

"Ignorant fool!" he snarled. "What know you of the eons of waiting—the warp and weft of the cosmic loom?"

For Mike and Hart, reality shattered in a blast of psychedelic waves—mind pain, psychic agony, deafening sound, followed by blindness and a suffocating vertigo. They yelled, rolling about with hands pressed to temples, mentally caught in a chaos of uprooted worlds.

∞

Duqayne gripped into the battle on a deeper level, in the unmeasured abyss of that Limbo where space and time are one. But now the dark was riven by the metallic blue nova glare of ultimate psychic forces, cross-whipped and thrust through by triple and quadruple opponents. A hall of mirrors, odd-angled translucent planes to Infinity, dimensionless yet all-encompassing. He smelled and saw the scaled Nephilim, the aged troglodyte Overlord demon writhing and clawing from a thousand points around him —yet simultaneously he embraced his love in the coven below. The spirit nakedness of Ariadne, the witchfire of nymph-succubus Melusina, the brother satyr grip of Cyprian—all of them locked in an intimacy beyond the flesh, in a soul-continuum of welded ego-strength, in a float of other summoned eyes that saw but could not strike.

"Eko, Eko Azarak!"

Their cry of dredged-up martial wrath from the triangle and the inverted pentagram, the witch and warlock hate stored up for days in the waning moon against the coming of the Beast.

"Droch! Mirroch! Esanaroth!"

Naked but for witch's bridles and goggles of dicyanin, they loped with him in powerful symbolic charge through mental plains of night, reeking their death of Saturnian bane, of blackthorn leaves and sulphur, of nettles and dwale and mandrake root—conjuring their vortex of darkness in the vales of Cernunnas and Habondia, in the funereal glades of Noticula, Lady of Night.

The monster bellowing, looming in the form of the Minotaur, that hideous son of Pasiphae where Theseus led the children of Athens from the Daedelean Labyrinth. They hurled their molten chains to bind him and he stood bewildered against them—the atavistic death face staring, the burning eyes of hellfire—his counter-wave of crushing lament, the ancient anguish and cries of Titan longing out of Elysian spheres a million years removed—the old threat of monster hate and destruction, again the aged giant-knowledge and tired star-wisdom, now falling in fiery shards. He could not blast their cone of force. Their psychic thrusts were strangely augmented as they welled beyond the pentacle. The demon staggered back in startled wrath.

Through the multiple veils of the cross-planed continuum they could dimly see the outer reality also—the hallway, and Brock staggering up over the prostrate forms of Mike and Hart. The senator figure had made it to the study doorway and stood there now with half-shattered screen, a living superimposure of horror—now man, now giant shadow of gleaming demonic form, moaning through echoing mental distances in his colossal rage, but starting to fall back.

Through the front door came the furious "O"-man, yelling against psychic pain, dropping to a knee and renting the study doorway with raving lead from an M-15.

Their force cone had to hold even though the monster retreated. But Stanger had ripped and shattered the thing's mortal host, who stiffened in death and fell forward to the floor, briefly losing the features of Cain, to be replaced by the face of the missing Wishnow—then finally shriveling into a mummified corpse whose hollow eyes stared into a lake of blood.

The demon had fled. Duqayne knew that his own physical body clutched the staircase railing for support, yet for a lingering, fading moment he was still in the pentacle ring with its haze of incense and candles. Lillian swooning at last from her efforts, and Melusina and Cyprian sinking exhausted to their knees among their chosen coven.

Even as he swam into merciful oblivion he saw the special cameras, the video equipment still at work, the dicyanin filters on the infra recorders—still heard the subliminal music, still tasted the ionized gases that the psychopharmacologists had provided. . . .

∞

Dimly, Duqayne perceived many voices around him. He sensed intuitively that he was recovering slowly from a severe reaction—the convalescence from the operation, the loss of blood, the bullet extraction, and the superhuman drain on his psyche. Physical, mental, and spiritual depletion had been followed by chills and fever. In welcome lethargy he had listened spasmodically, the occasional wisps of conversation touching him only vagluely in passing. But as he lay there in the luxury of a Hart mansion bedroom, he learned much more from the prevailing patterns of thought.

The "O"-man's amulet . . . probably jimmied by Thane. Psychokinesis. Stanger, not thrown far enough by the teleportation, had made it back in time. And then there were the arguments about the Bug. It had somehow permitted a delay of the ultimate commitment in order to allow a completion of the experiment in the basement—for two basic reasons: scientific support of paranormal techniques at this point was of vital importance; and that which superseded X was the advent of himself, David Duqayne. The coven had formed a "bridge" through which he had teleported.

He learned that government priority and a financial carte blanche from Omega had collected an impressive array of world authorities in the field of the paranormal sciences, along with their more portable equipment. This was the concession that Lillian had demanded in return for being an Alpha decoy. She knew that if she were going to make a try to find him she would need all the help she could get. Moreover, should the attempt succeed in some measurable degree, the phenomenon would be recorded officially. Such an achievement would then support the establishment of the world's first tactical paragnostic unit —the Omega *Psi*-Corps. Duqayne had been Lillian's prime concern; the arrangement had mainly been the pricetag of collaboration by Cyprian and Melusina. And Duqayne was secretly sensing that this Cyprian was as much of a "growing boy" as the Bug itself— perhaps with much more independent ideas. Still playing the "magician."

When he felt strong enough to let them know it, the crowd in the bedroom had dwindled down to a baker's dozen. Aside from a few professional myopic types who were strangers, plus the Pentagon general and his aide, there were Lillian, Mike, Hart, Brockway, Stanger, Ascot, and Cyprian and Melusina—the latter now once more in the hippie role of Larry and Heidi.

Lillian cried out and rushed to him in a warm wave of soft female essence and love. The golden elixir might have penetrated but for the general's next words.

"As the President has put it, gentlemen, there is your super-weapon!"

Dave got up on his elbows, glaring. Lillian buried her head against his shoulder, starting to cry. "Don't cut me out, David!" she whispered.

Mike Havelin drew heavily on his pipe at the foot of the bed, with Hart and Brockway catching the poignant innuendoes.

He tried to mutter to her privately: "The wedding bells have *cracked*, Lil. They'll jangle the unholiest tune you've ever heard if I touch them—ever again!"

She tried to run out of the room. Mike simply blocked her and took over. He held her to him, stroking her dark long hair, letting her know she could cry it all out and tell the world to go to hell.

Dave fought against baring his soul. Had to keep all the kind hearts and gentle people out of the impact area! The soft music and wine and candlelight were way off somewhere in another dimension.

"What's the matter with all of you!" he shouted at the silent faces. "Can't you read the blood on the wall?"

Friends only stared. Brockway and Cyprian seemed to *really* comprehend. As for Melusina—tears for Lillian and Mike. . . .

Later, the President was on the phone and you couldn't say no to that if you were dying. Congressional medal and all.

"We're sorry we had to give so many people a jolt about the Box," said the Chief Executive. "When it was discovered that it had disappeared, all of you must have really panicked."

"Teleportation," commented Duqayne with seeming listlessness. "Thane took it along with him. It was his plan from the start, masquerading as Cain."

"Of course! But not the real thing! At the time, only the Bug itself knew the truth. But after all now, everybody should have realized we wouldn't expose the *actual* Box to the enemy like that! It was only a near-perfect facsimile of *X*. Let them waste their time on it as long as they please. Right?"

Duqayne delayed his answer for quite a long moment, still hearing the somber words of the demon: *"What know you of the eons of waiting—the warp and weft of the cosmic loom?"*

Abruptly he switched his levels and answered. "Yes, sir. I mean—you're right, sir. . . ."

The morning sun slanted warmly through the open curtains. Duqayne heard the song of a bird. He got out of bed and went to the window, gazing downward at the green Bel-Air hills. He felt physically regenerated but there was a stagnation and bitterness of the soul—a taste of despair, a black iron chain of final resignation. He must submit.

All right, so it was the new beginning, and what were the facts? There were few people, if any, who could comprehend the awesome magnitude of his perceptions now. Certainly not the President or his cabinet or the Joint Chiefs, or even the Omega Council or Hart, himself.

But what of the lingering enigma, Irving Brockway? In the final desperate thrust at the demon, whence had come that saving surge of *outside* power? The Brockway who had controlled the minds of Hart and Mike and Lillian that night in the factory penthouse had surely been Thane in one of his masquerades. But the Brockway who had *known* that Cain was the demon in disguise, and who had retained his faculties when Mike and Hart were writhing on the floor—who was he? A probe of his mind had instantly revealed a perfect innocence—in fact *too* instantly and *too* perfect. There was much that was yet to be told.

With the advent of a new model of the universe, the stability of normal human reason was threatened. Even those at the top had to be at least partially shielded from the growing reality *behind* the reality of interlocked Other Dimensions and parallel universes. The human psyche had its defense mechanisms, forever constructing a mythological screen between itself and a reality that said Man-on-Earth was *not* supreme. The ego couldn't take it—not without cracking up, or not without hate and desperate destructions.

But the facts were as monolithic and enduring as the planet's core. The K-Man star descendants *had* come "in unto the daughters of men." Duqayne had sensed things in his brief contact with the demon, things that the monster had deliberately sought to convey—as though to say: If you do come against us, remember *this!* That strange poignancy of epic lamentation, the dim and distant vista of those Elysian spheres lost somewhere, somewhen, in the vastness of the Greater Continuum. What was their *real* story? And where was Evil or Good? Were these unknown superbeings another form of archangels, and Man himself the denizen of Hell?

As for the Box, there was the greatest burden of all. Like a Sixth Estate, the new invisible government protected the trusting public from even the knowledge of its existence and what it portended. In their own self-righteousness they judged that which was good or bad for their wards. But should *he* continue to protect these upper echelons of leadership, including Omega itself, solely on his own recognizance? In whom could he confide?

A small sparrow alighted on the sill outside the open window. It perched there unsuspectingly and preened itself in the sun. There was no one else, so he confided in it. How could he tell them they had been fooled? Thane's perfect plan had resulted in Stanger's preconditioning even before the Box was switched. That which sat in a subterranean vault at the Lodge *was* the ingenious facsimile. The real X was elsewhere—and now only he and the sparrow knew. They had to be prepared for such a shock lest the Bug launch an Omega One, thus destroying their gains before they could use them. Before he could tell them, he had to prepare himself with further knowledge so as to give them hope instead of despair.

"I didn't *ask* for this!" he muttered half aloud.

Startled, the bird hopped along the ledge, finally

aware of his presence. But like Castiglia's "Fatted Calf," it was chubby from friendly feedings in the park. Duqayne aimed a thought at the tiny piece of fluff: *"I killed a bird once—are you not afraid, little one?"*

The bird continued to preen. Duqayne's lethal forces gathered experimentally, darkly roiling against his bitter plight—but in the last moment he desisted. The bird took flight, blissfully unaware that its small heart still functioned by the grace of a monster's will.

A lonely world . . . forever dark and lonely. *This* one, anyway. But what of Elysian spheres beyond?

After all, there was *X*. Only the classical hero deed remained—to enter forbidden realms and wrest it from Titan hands. In that Pandora's box, in that goodie bag of the gods with all its pricetags—*there* lay his golden wings . . . !

THE END